THE
GREAT STATE
OF WEST FLORIDA

Also by Kent Wascom

The New Inheritors
Secessia
The Blood of Heaven

THE
GREAT STATE
OF **WEST
FLORIDA**

a novel

KENT
WASCOM

Black Cat
New York

FIRST EDITION

Published simultaneously in Canada
Printed in the United States of America

First Grove Atlantic paperback edition: May 2024

Library of Congress Cataloging-in-Publication data is available for this title.

ISBN 978-0-8021-6284-7
eISBN 978-0-8021-6285-4

Black Cat
an imprint of Grove Atlantic
154 West 14th Street
New York, NY 10011

Distributed by Publishers Group West

groveatlantic.com

24 25 26 27   10 9 8 7 6 5 4 3 2 1

For Alise

Belief has nothing to do with true or false.
Never has. Never will.

—Harry Crews

THE
GREAT STATE
OF WEST
FLORIDA

THE BATTLE OF TIGER COVE

Now she rides the highways and the spurs, making stops from town to town along the coast. You might've seen her mean white pony car parked up in some vacant lot or on the margins of a strip mall's crowded blacktop, window down, her gleaming elbow cocked, handing out notes of currency with the name we call her by now and the name of our state and a whole lot of zeros on them. She says she has millions and millions more. She says she'll come again and when she does, you can cash the notes for precious metals, End Times loot, and if you didn't believe her already, all you had to do was look and see yourself reflected in the gold electroplating of her arm, the metal casing engraved with intricate wave forms and scenes and foliate scrollwork like an old-time quickdraw pistol.

There you are, in the glow of summer eternal, and you might've been a loser all your life, been fucked on and ignored, but slip that bill in your pocket and swear your oath, because you're a West Floridian now, and everything's gonna be different.

But it wasn't always like this.

Time was, she didn't have any money to give, with her name on it or not. Time was, she didn't have but one name that anybody alive called her. Didn't have but one arm. Didn't have too long to live, it seemed.

A time called 2013 in a place they still called Florida.

While the battle raged downstairs, Destiny Woolsack zipped the collar of the biker jacket and fastened it across her throat with a strap of leather and a brass button that went pop. Eighteen years old and crouched between sloping roof beams and the keepsake bins and the garbage bags of her mother's exes' things. Screams like storm surge rising from the rooms below. Motes of fiberglass insulation trembling in the light of a lone bulb. A glittery pink haze on the heat-choked air. She breathed as deep as she could and took a racing helmet from one of the bags and made her way across the joists to the door of the attic loft where she'd been hiding since the Florida Wars began, about five minutes back.

You could go further off into history if you wanted and find a lot of other battles that predated this one, a lot of killings and hostile encounters, or you could look ahead and see more glaring recent incidents, which we'll get to in good time, but for my money, for my family, this is where it all starts.

She listened at the door in the attic floor. Howls and babbling from downstairs. Crashing glass. Something hard being slammed into something soft, over and over again. With her right and only arm she pulled the busted racing helmet on, a black Arai detailed in cherry red, its visor all scratched up from some old vintage wreck. Like the jacket, like the boots, like the glove she'd pulled on with her teeth, the helmet had belonged to her mom's ex-boyfriend Deke, and the foam against her face stank of beer sweat and the turn of the millennium, but it was better armor than nothing.

She told herself she was a trooper set to leap out of the belly of a plane. Because this was a battle, not like what they'd say later on, before the truth came out. For most people, for the longest time, what happened in her house was just some bloodbath home invasion off the twelfth-hole fairway of a Jerry Pate signature course. The Gulf Breeze Massacre. And there's some who still believe that mess, who even now will lay the blame squarely on the shoulders of this girl right here, the one in the helmet and the jacket, about to lower the attic door into hell on earth.

She'd been up there rifling through the bags of Deke's stuff, looking for things she might sell to finance the life she'd never have now. She'd already gone through her mom's shit in the bedroom closet below, took some money and pills, and her next stop was the bins where her step-grandma Krista kept the memorabilia from her brief career as a Miss Hawaiian Tropic Pensacola Beach and a straight-to-video actress—sashes and magazines and a black satin *Scream Queens* jacket—then the plan had been to move on to her long-dead Pawpaw's stuff in the master bedroom across the landing, get a couple high-ticket items stashed while the rest of the family was downstairs smoking, watching TV, reading their phones. Once they'd all passed out or gone to bed, she'd slip down and get her keys and some credit cards and leave their sorry asses forever.

Then came the shouts and the screams and before she could think, before she could do anything else, she'd pulled the door shut and crouched there, listening to her people die.

Her mom and Krista.

The boys, Kenan and Rodney.

Like she'd wished it on them.

At first, she could tell their voices apart as each one sang out horribly in alarm or confusion, like they could stop it by shouting hey, no, wait. When this still seemed like a robbery, before the killing began. Then their voices braided, melted, became as confused as her own genealogy and life here with her mom, Alexis, and Krista, who was technically her step-grandmother, even though Krista was basically the same age as her mom, and Krista's sons, who were technically her uncles, if they were even still alive anymore.

She'd been all set to go, too. On the verge of freedom. That's partly why they first blamed her—because Destiny had some shit-ass friends who afterwards would tell the reporters that she'd been talking a lot lately about being gone, being free, and how she'd always been, let's say, intense, so you had to take her at her word. Now, they didn't want you to get the wrong idea, these rising seniors, and they recalled moments such as Destiny on the Quietwater Beach Boardwalk their sophomore year climbing up into the blush-colored scallop band shell and belting out an honestly heartbreaking rendition of the reprise of "Part of Your World." Tears were seen in eyes from there to Hooters. She just hadn't been the same since the accident, they said. She'd always said she was leaving first chance she got, but once she lost her arm it went from teenage venom to solemn vow that she was done with those motherfuckers, her family. And since among the three cranked-up killers who busted in on them was her half aunt Tara, Pawpaw's own eldest daughter from his first marriage, and because another of them was Nessa Pace, ex-girlfriend and mother of the child of her technical uncle Kenan, and because Nessa was a former classmate of Destiny's at De Luna High, people were inclined to believe she was in on the whole thing. Maybe left the door unlocked. A plan gone horribly wrong.

Never mind she hadn't so much as met her half aunt Tara, only knew her as somebody her mom would admit in sad introspective moments to having fucked over pretty badly long ago. Never mind that she and her technical uncle Kenan's ex-girlfriend Nessa Pace had been sworn enemies at school. When you come down to it, people want to believe what makes them feel better, and nothing makes people feel better than the idea that the victims of violence are somehow the authors of their own misfortune.

The other reason folks got the idea Destiny might have been somehow involved, or at best ran off and left her family to their fate, was because when the night was over and the bodies were accounted, hers wasn't among them.

The fucked-up thing was, she could've left them there, could've busted the attic window and crawled onto the roof and slid down the jasmine trellis, risked maybe a broken wrist or ankle, and ran off into the night.

Who could blame her? If you went by the stats on the back of her blister pack, she shouldn't have stood a chance.

She was on the short side, and spread around her in this house were three deranged intruders armed with guns, knives, and other instruments of death. Her bio might say she was born in Baton Rouge in 1995. Might say she lost her left arm a little over a year ago in an accident caused by her mom, who was trying to chase down a hit-and-run driver on Highway 98 in Deke's truck. Might say Deke's dead body, wrapped around a guardrail below a Ron Jon Surf Shop sign, was the first corpse she ever saw, though it wouldn't be the last. Rank: fuckup first and only daughter, pseudosister to her uncles, aged fifteen and thirteen. Currently attending Florida Virtual School, a fifth-year senior but not for lack of smarts. The little grid row indicating that particular stat would be about halfway full. Strength? Some. Speed? Medium. Firepower? None, at the moment. In terms of toughness, though, she'd spent the summer punching hot cinders in the backyard Weber, and when it came to courage, well, on that night those little rectangular motherfuckers would be full and blazing red all the way to the end of the row.

So she lowered the spring-loaded door and stepped down the rungs onto the soft white pile carpet of her mom's bedroom in too-big ankle boots and stood there for a moment, trying not to hear what was happening downstairs or the quaking bed frame and the barking grunts coming from the master bedroom across the landing, not thirty feet away.

Because courage and toughness don't mean much when you're outnumbered and outgunned. What she needed now were weapons, and she knew just where to look.

Under the bed in the master bedroom, where something terrible was happening, tucked inside a Dillard's shoebox, was a pair of Crown Royal bags. One held a big black Colt Police revolver and the other a fistful of fat brass .38 Special cartridges. She knew this because her whole life she'd been going in there and drawing that pistol for fun and comfort. Dim afternoons with the blinds drawn, hefting its weight, trying to learn the action. To perfect the border shift or the Curly Bill spin. Pawpaw had called the gun his Dirty Harry, though it'd come from the days of the Depression, really, and an uncle of his who'd been a sheriff's deputy before he got sent to prison on some bullshit dug up by a *Times-Picayune* reporter. Years later, faced with his own prison term for conspiracy and fraud and money laundering, Pawpaw had made his third wife Krista promise to keep the Colt safe and cleaned and oiled. And she had, through the fourteen months he spent at Saufley Field, just down the road in Pensacola, and then the years following his escape and flight and capture and resentencing, when he was sent off to Three Rivers Correctional out in Del Rio, Texas, the very same federal facility that the sons of bitches had sent his uncle to back in the seventies.

She thought of the revolver. Between her hand and its Franzite grip was an open loft on the landing, a game room with a pool table and a hoop on the wall for foam basketballs and beside that her Pawpaw's Big Chief quarter-payout slot machine, a gift back in the day from some New Orleans gangster's son, he'd told her once.

Pawpaw told her a lot of things. About herself, about West Florida, which was just some history shit before he'd gotten ahold of it. He'd taken a footnote and turned it into a real place and state of mind for listeners across the Gulf Coast. They'd tuned in to his radio show, self-professed patriots who couldn't believe in their country anymore, so he gave them a land they could believe in, a country inside the country, that'd always been theirs, always would be, a place they could reclaim, remake into somewhere the government couldn't run up and Ruby Ridge you. By the time his audience peaked in the midnineties, he was selling West Florida on shares, bought land and built a mansion and the beginning of what was supposed to be some kind of antigovernment settlement out in Garcon Point, across the bay from Gulf Breeze, before the feds caught up to him. Pawpaw told her about that property and the mansion and everything that should've been theirs. He told her what he'd planned for West Florida, what could've been, and while the boys played with other inmates' kids in the outside area and their mothers sat spreading cream cheese on vending machine bagels, he and Destiny drew maps and plans of that would-be state on coarse brown visiting-room napkins. He marveled at this girl, her steeliness and command, how easily bossing came to her. Pretty soon she was telling him where things should go and how they ought to be. That's when he started calling her the Governor. What he thought, deep down, he could've been, if everything hadn't gone sideways. He was the first to call her by that name and for many years no one else would.

He told her she was bound for greatness, as if her given name wasn't enough. He told her about the double-action trigger of the Colt. The way it hesitated at the end of the stroke. He told her men weren't worth a shit when you came down to it, so never trust one with your heart, but she knew that already. What he didn't tell her whenever they'd visit him out in Del Rio, her mom or her step-grandma Krista filled in on the way. Her jacked-up lineage rolling by like roadside attractions while she stretched unbelted in the back seat and sipped on a blue raspberry Slush Puppie.

The last thing Pawpaw told her was, OK, he didn't have to call her the Governor anymore, if that was what she wanted. Destiny was twelve, and what she wanted was to be done with pretend. Pawpaw sat across from her with wet eyes, forcing a smile, and not long after, he was dead. They drove out to Texas to retrieve a jarful of ashes on their last big family prison road trip. They poured him out at various crucial points along I-10 on their way home while Destiny sat in the back seething, trying to hide her guilt with rage.

She hadn't thought of herself as the Governor in years, and she wasn't destined for a damn thing except an awful death, it looked like. She'd become a fuckhead kid who'd spit in the face of the only person who'd ever really believed in her and had planned that night to steal his Colt revolver and sell it too.

Destiny didn't want to be that kid, any more than she wanted to be dead.

So she became who she was always meant to be.

Looking out the scarred and road-burnt visor of the racing helmet, she saw everything through a crimson mist, the atmosphere of a planet with gunpowder sands and bloodred skies lit by a sun called Hell. She went across the room to her mom's dresser and opened the sock drawer and filtered through a sea of balled up no-shows until she finally found a pair that were calf length. She shook one sock loose, slipped it in her jacket pocket, and went out into the game room.

Screams tore up the stairwell's throat. She crossed the landing and came to the pool table and ran her hand along the scuffed baize rail and reached into the side pocket and palmed up a billiard ball and slipped it into her jacket. She squatted beneath the basketball hoop, in the chrome-plated shadow of the slot machine, the Big Chief's brass head the size of a trailer hitch watching over her while she worked the ball into the mouth of the sock.

This accomplished, she stood and took the sock by its neck and swung it once in a circle so the ball settled in the toe, and she headed for the master bedroom.

When they'd been younger, right here, she'd seen Rodney go up for a dunk on his big brother, Kenan, who upended him and smashed Rodney's foot against the Big Chief's head so that Rodney fell and lay there clutching his leg, sobbing in pain. The same kinds of sounds she heard now coming from the other side of the door. Only worse.

She toed the door aside and stepped into the room, whipping the billiard ball hip-high. Outside, in the shallows of the Santa Rosa Sound, bull sharks swam inshore to breed the next relentless generation there in razored sands.

The man in the bedroom was enormous and naked to the waist. A lineman's bulk inked with snaking nooses and black-letter maxims. He had his back to her and his mind on the awful shit he was doing to Rodney on the bed with the boning knife in his hand, so he didn't turn at her approach. Then it was too late, and his mind was on what the hell had just happened, and why couldn't he see too good, and what was this half-inch-deep crater doing in his skull. She swung again. Blood spray on the valance, Rodney—to her shock—alive and crawling away to the bathroom, where he locked himself in and slumped against the door and passed out. Now the dent-skulled man caught himself in the window frame and came slashing at her with his knife. She backed up and the blade glanced off her helmet and the man kept coming, cut a six-inch gash in the black leather of the biker jacket. When he came at her again she was ready and the ball shattered his elbow. He bent double, still holding the knife, and let off a cry that reminded her of a kid she used to babysit, how he'd wail when he didn't get what he wanted, and she raised her makeshift flail again, windmilling, so that the man's eyes couldn't help but follow the ball until the fatal moment when it crushed his temple and she brought the ball back around and his mind was all over everything.

The sock hung sopping, heavy at her side. She squeezed it and, hearing the dying man's glutch and groan, she went to where he'd fallen, curled, trying to protect what was left of his head. She squatted over him and hit him again and again. Her swings went wild, busted the drywall, cracked the baseboard. When the man was quiet and she finally let her weapon go it landed with a wet thud on the rug. For a moment she stood with her fist clenched, awaiting the sound of footsteps on the stairs, and when none came she went quickly to the bathroom door and pressed her hand to the stile. Told the boy on the other side it was gonna be over soon, she was here now, and she'd be back. Her words muffled by the helmet, half-true. Things like this are never over, and the bull sharks bred in the waters of the sound that night would grow and mate and bear live young themselves before she saw him again.

She knelt beside the mattress and lifted the bed skirt and dug beneath the frame until her fingers found the Dillard's shoebox. She pulled the box out and lifted the silver lid, parted the tissue paper, revealing the gold and purple glory of the whiskey bags. Tears welling, she spread one bag's puckered mouth wide and let the .38 slide into her lap. She took the pistol up and tested it in her gloved grip. Her finger bulky in the trigger guard. The Governor thumbed the cylinder release and opened the bag of cartridges and loaded six and snapped the cylinder back and before she headed downstairs she looped her thumb in the golden drawstring and cinched the bag of ammunition and pocketed it as she rose magnificent with the Colt in her hand.

CHAPTER ONE

CALL ME MURDERBABY

Welcome to West Florida, population my family and me and about a million and a half other people, more or less.

I guess we're what you'd call the first family of the state, the Woolsacks, unless you call us criminals or enemies or crazy-ass coast trash on a spree. The Governor says that here we're free to be our true bad selves, and that's what West Florida means to her. Then again, Leona O., who owns my heart forever, says I'm all the state she'll ever need, says I'm enough to fight for, wherever we are.

That's the thing about West Florida: you might say it's the ten counties and a little under two hundred miles of crystal sand and marsh and pineland that stretch from the Rio Perdido to Apalachicola, or you could say it's just a dream. You could say it's everything from the Mississippi north of New Orleans and on under the thirty-first parallel to down around the Big Bend, or you could say if there ever was a real West Florida it's long dead now. You could call it a bastion of liberty, the last free place, like Troy Yarbrough's people do, when what they really mean is a Jesus-riddled white ethnostate with a beachside pastel tinge. You could say it's the unending glory of an awesome summer in which all our people have the right to be who and what they are, like the Governor says. You could say anything, including you've never heard of it till now.

Nothing wrong with that.

Me, I'm at the heart of this whole thing and I was almost thirteen years old before I heard of West Florida, and I'd been living here my whole entire life.

If you'd asked me back then, I would've said I lived in the Beau Rivage subdivision in Mandeville, Louisiana, with my Aunt Amber, until she died, and her husband Big Mike and their twin boys, Dakota James and Dakota Blake, named for the state where Big Mike made his money in the Bakken boom, before he and Amber got into the payday loan business. And if you'd asked them, they would've said I was the Murderbaby.

My mom, Nessa Pace, was Amber's sister, and so she'd taken me in after I was found as a six-month infant heat-stroking in the back seat of a car parked behind the house where the quote-unquote Gulf Breeze Massacre had taken place. My mom's car, to be exact. By the time Amber had collected me and brought me to live with them, Big Mike and his boys had already saddled me with the name.

Amber and Big Mike didn't believe in keeping things from kids, no matter how little you were. They took great pride in telling it how it was, admired those who claimed to do the same, wore shirts explaining in list form their lack of filter, fucks given, and other traits. And according to them, when it came to me, the way it was, was this: My mom and Amber had grown up in Pensacola, even though their roots were here, in Louisiana, which Amber'd had the good sense to go back to as soon as she could, and she'd been genuinely happy for her little sister when she heard that Nessa was all eaten up with this boy named Kenan Woolsack, whose family, wouldn't you know it, also had roots in Louisiana. Only their roots were all gnarled up and contaminated from leach water and probably ran through gas lines, and even though they had money his family were themselves the kind of reckless fuckheads who'd dig in their yard without calling the utility company and blow up a neighbor's house or two on accident. A family of single moms and future single moms and boys who'd turn perfectly good girls into single moms.

Which is exactly what happened to my mom, according to Amber and Big Mike, and when it did, this kid Kenan not only dumped her, not only denied everything for months, but he wouldn't even face her when she showed up, bump and all, at their door. Instead, his mom, Krista, and her stepdaughter,

Alexis, and *her* daughter, Destiny, all got in my now-single mom's face and said if they ever caught her on their property again they'd, well, do some criminal-ass shit. Had the nerve, when Nessa didn't budge, to start in about the boy Kenan being too young for her, how she'd taken advantage of him. Which Amber always said was a bullshit excuse, and I guessed it was, but later when I did the math I saw he would've been heading into ninth grade that year and she a junior in high school. Regardless, my mom dropped out and had me, and Kenan would never make it to sophomore year. My mom ended up in Louisiana, where Amber and Big Mike could keep tabs on her, help her with bills and baby stuff, but she grew desperate and also addicted to drugs: Big Mike called it the despair that was killing white people, a phrase he'd heard some pundit say, which he went on repeating and applying to subsequent tragic deaths, including that of poor Aunt Amber, who went down as a result of fent.

The massacre happened because Nessa, my mom, kept scrolling through Facebook or Instagram and seeing these posts of Krista and Alexis, the ones who'd threatened her, denied her child, talking about how blessed they were and looking like the queens of summer. She shouldn't have been doing it, Amber said, but my mom wouldn't quit stalking the Woolsack women online and the Woolsack women wouldn't stop posting themselves sunning beside their pool or leaning against new cars, and my mom, she started screenshotting the posts and sharing them, talking about how bad they'd treated her, and then one of those things happened: the kind that get people fucked up and believing in fate.

One of Nessa's posts got shared outside her circle, liked for its fury against bitches who cover for their punk-ass sons, bitches who don't deserve what they got and if there's any justice in this world should get what they deserve, and the post was liked and shared until it ended up in the hands of one Tara Woolsack, whose half sister Alexis had left her to do six years in Elayn Hunt Correctional for attempted-murdering this guy they were going to rob back in the day. Six years while Alexis walked free and went off to live with her dad's third wife on the motherfucking beach.

DMs were sent. Meetings held. Meth smoked. Weaponry arranged. A pistol-grip pump shotgun and a pair of Glock 15s with auto switches and a set of metal knuckles with these long, sharp Wolverine claws that Tara kept behind the counter at the vape shop where she worked. At first it was just something to make themselves feel better, Nessa and Tara and Blake, the guy Tara had attempted to murder and who she'd later married because life and love are strange, talking big about what they'd do, and then it became a plan and the plan was to get in there and steal some shit, including cash and a big old sheaf of bonds Pawpaw had supposedly stashed before he went inside. That's what Nessa told Amber, before she left. They weren't going in there trying to kill anybody. Maybe terrorize the shit out of them, she said, but not kill.

She'd confessed the whole thing to Amber in a single raging burst one night when I was six months old and wouldn't sleep for nothing. Gave her a whole speech with me squalling in her arms. Amber told me later she tried to get her little sister to at least leave me there with her, where I'd be safe. Said when she asked my mom to do that, Nessa had glared at her with all the hatred in the world. Safe? she said, getting right up in Amber's face. You saying my baby isn't safe with me? Like I'm what? Dangerous? Well I'm a great fucking mom *because* I'm dangerous. Nothing's ever getting between me and my baby, understand me? And pretty soon, me and him, we're gonna get everything we're owed.

Amber didn't say anything back. Just watched her sister go.

By dawn Nessa had me in my little totable car seat on the road trip to the massacre.

I don't know what she was thinking, what kind of future she envisioned. Maybe she saw herself as some baby cart assassin, thought that I'd grow up admiring her vengeance, or maybe she thought she'd take my dad as a gunpoint bridegroom, and reveal it all to me years later when we were celebrating their umpteenth anniversary.

I don't know, but there I was: a baby riding along with a carload of maniacs slamming down the interstate to Gulf Breeze, Tiger Cove, where my mom and her accomplices would try to settle their scores, only to end up getting notched themselves.

Not to say they didn't do some damage first.

On the morning after the massacre, the responding officers discovered Rodney, the surviving boy, locked in the master
bathroom, to which he'd made his escape after being taken
to the master bedroom, assaulted, and stabbed a number of
times. To get there, the officers first had to follow a trail of
gore through the house, accounting for the two women resi-
dents, Krista Woolsack and Alexis Woolsack, the body of Kenan
Woolsack in the laundry room with his head in Nessa's lap,
she dead by gunshot wounds to the chest, and the attackers
scattered throughout in attitudes of struggle, a fight amongst
themselves perhaps, a freakout that left my mom and the
other perpetrators dead.

Back when I was still ashamed of her, I liked to think
that's how it went. Like my mom had been killed by one of
her accomplices, shot maybe because in the midst of whatever
awful shit was happening she found herself filled suddenly
with regret and tried to take it back, like when you're little
and you hit somebody and they start crying and all your rage
dries up and you want to stuff all their tears back in their eyes,
even though of course you can't.

That's not how it happened, though. I wouldn't learn the
whole truth until later, the details Amber and Big Mike didn't
know or the Dakotas couldn't cook up or I myself couldn't
find in the articles I read once I had enough sense to google it
or in the true crime forum threads I checked on for a while,
where people geeked out over the whole thing.

Like I said, I had a lot to learn. And a lot to unlearn, too.

Back then all anybody knew was that the girl, Destiny, was a missing person, status unknown. They found her Toyota in the driveway and her keys hanging from the flamingo wall-hook. The only clue she'd left was a trail of bloody footprints leading out of the house and down the driveway, articles of clothing strung in the reeds of the vacant lot across the street that ended at the shoreline, like she'd walked out of that Armageddon house and disappeared into the dawn-lit waters of the Santa Rosa Sound.

The people on the true crime forums posted theories and updates and unconfirmed sightings of Destiny for years. You had your she-was-in-on-it people and your ones who thought she survived and was wild and free and wandering the woods like Jeremiah fucking Johnson, who some say is dead and some say never will be, and others who said she died and got tossed into the water and was devoured by sea life. Mostly what seemed to hold their attention was the idea that she'd been in on it and double-crossed and trafficked into sexual slavery by heretofore unknown accomplices who'd somehow escaped detection by the forensics team. You could tell by the posts this was the version their hearts beat hardest for, the version where they knew more and better than the people who'd picked through the gore and numbered the entry wounds and shell casings, the version with an eternal victim in permanent pain.

I never bought that, me.

For most of my life, Destiny was a ghost, a nightmare, something to fear.

When I was little, the Dakotas would say she was coming for me. They'd say she was crab-crawling through the halls of our house at night so I stayed glued to my bed. Say if it was storming and I dared to part the blinds, she'd be standing there pressed up against the wet window, peering in, a vengeful spirit with no one left to take it out on, no one left to kill, except a murderbaby like me.

Didn't matter to her that it wasn't my fault or that I was barely alive when it happened. Probably the only reason she'd spared me that night when I was a baby, walked right past the car where I sat with the windows rolled up, crying in the heat, was because she was saving me for last, waiting until I'd grown and sinned enough to earn whatever hell she had in store for me.

The weird thing is, out of everybody's theories, theirs was closest to the truth.

Even still, I never should've believed the Dakotas, considering these were the same brothers who'd once talked me into placing my fat little toddler hand on the overheated engine of their go-kart so that when Amber finally came out and took me by the shoulder and yanked me away, my palm came off like pizza cheese. But I believed them. I mean, I'd be lying if I didn't say there were times when the Dakotas felt like brothers to me, times I held onto hard the fewer and farther between they got to be. And I'd be lying if I didn't say I held out hope that they'd one day remember those times too, and take me under their Realtree-decked wings, but that was back when Amber was alive. When she died of the despair, her sons turned meaner than before. Not that I blame them much. They're the ones who found her on the bathroom floor.

If I miss any of them, I miss Aunt Amber.

She was the only one I'd eat with.

At the time I had this thing where I didn't like to eat in front of people, especially the Dakotas and their dad, or kids at school, or in restaurants. Late at night, when Big Mike was asleep or out and the Dakotas were up in their room screaming into their headsets, I'd go down and sit with Amber and together on the couch we'd eat in peace and comfort, not having to hear that the way you've arranged your legs under yourself is gay, or that what you're eating is making you soft, which in Big Mike's lexicon could mean gay or fat and to him I was both.

Which isn't the worst thing somebody can say when you've got rolls and there's been rumors about you since you were in third grade and you contracted meningitis. I was friends with this kid Braiden Cartier at the time. We played together during aftercare. As tight as it gets for little kids. I was smaller and weirder and he was very tall and perfect-haired and would only grow taller and more perfect in various ways later on. When I got sick, at first it was unknown whether I had viral (bad) or bacterial (worse) meningitis, until I wound up in

Lakeview Regional, where they gave me a spinal tap. But before that happened, Amber and Mike, who I still called Mommy and Daddy, sat there and asked me if I'd maybe shared a drink or some food with Braiden at lunch or aftercare. Then a doctor and a nurse came in and asked the same thing. Which I denied because ew, gross, I wouldn't share a drink or food with anyone, even Braiden, and also because what is this, 1988, and we're all drinking out of the proverbial hose. Regardless, these adults heard me say no in a small sick voice and they did not believe me. They could not possibly have believed me, I know, and I couldn't possibly ever think of them like a mom and dad again, because of what happened next.

The doctor then asked had I ever *kissed* Braiden Cartier. Bad enough being asked by medical professionals if you had kissed another boy, but then Big Mike shoved in talking about, Did that boy touch you, did he put his mouth on you? This was his version of being a hero, but he didn't look like a hero, he looked like he was looking at something that belonged in what he called the commode but was sitting here unflushed on a hospital bed not telling the truth. Shortly afterwards I was given what is considered one of the most painful medical procedures going, which I've since learned cops administered to fucking serial murder suspects in the old days, to make them confess.

Well, I confessed everything I'd ever felt and many things I'd never done and by the time I got out of the hospital Big Mike and Amber and the Dakotas had spread it all around that I was gay. I tried to correct the record a couple of times, naively believing that if my peers and family understood I liked certain girls as much as I liked boys like Braiden Cartier then maybe they wouldn't find me so gross. Except to some people, especially my erstwhile family and apparently the certain girls whose names I'd given as proof that I wasn't totally gay, liking both is even worse.

I went on sneaking snacks at night with Amber, but it never felt safe in the same way again. Plus she was mostly gone on fent by then. She'd slip off for a while and come back to the couch and I'd look over and she'd be nodding, and some nights she wouldn't come back at all. You'd hear her wake up, *whump*, in the bathroom after you went to bed. Meanwhile, Big Mike would come back from the fishing camp or work or whatever and tell me I was getting softer. See me sipping a can of Delaware Punch and ask if any other lips than mine had kissed the rim. Catch me eating a candy bar and lay a whole new nickname on me. Butterfinger. Emphasis on the *butt* and the *finger*.

I didn't always just take it, though. I remember one time I bowed up, balled my fists and hiked my shoulders to my ears, and screamed in Big Mike's face that I hadn't been eating a fucking Butterfinger because I don't like how fucking Butterfingers stick up in your fucking teeth, OK? Well, I know how I looked because the Dakotas were filming and made damn sure I saw later how my eyes went pitiful when Big Mike's goatee closed around his mouth—pinched and hair-ringed as a monkey's sphincter—and he got down in my face real close, veins risen up his neck and into his forehead like pissed-off ants were tunneling through him, and said murderously slow that he knew for a fact my soft ass had been scarfing down a crispety-crunchety peanut-buttery Butterfinger, or was I calling him a liar in his goddamn house?

I remember seeing Amber over his shoulder, shaking her head at me like, No, don't. Just agree.

That was the shortest way to a quiet night: Just agree. Believe what someone else says about you, live in their reality no matter how wrong.

So I did—that time and all the others—until the very end.

I hate it, but I miss her. Even if she didn't stop anyone from calling me Murderbaby, or soft, and even if when she was upset she would cuss not just my supposed father and his whole fucked-up family, but her little sister too. Even if she let her boys use the specter of the vengeful Destiny to scare me. More and more, I think Amber wanted her out there like a warning, like people in the old days would use Rawhead and Bloody Bones to keep their kids from going near the water's edge.

Like maybe she could see West Florida looming on the horizon, waiting for me. I don't know. For all their telling it how it was, neither one of my caretakers ever told me the whole story. They never said my grandma Krista was in episodes of shows that ran on the USA Network, that she was in movies, real movies, even if they went straight to video and featured gratuitous bikini scenes and sharks edited together from other shark movies by unscrupulous Italian directors. And they never told me about Pawpaw either, or at least anything other than he'd gone to prison and had three or four wives. They didn't tell me he'd built a mansion and a neighborhood, the start of a whole new state, and had it all taken away. I don't think they were trying to be bad, at least with that part. Maybe nobody ever has the whole story about anything, and I don't think they knew much about the whole West Florida thing. Nobody did, really, until the spring of my last days in Mandeville, when that bastard Troy Yarbrough stole my Woolsack family's whole idea.

Back then, when I still went to school in what I thought was Louisiana, we had this teacher who wanted to know what we'd do if there was another civil war. Had us take this question home. This was after State Rep. Troy Yarbrough and his bill to create a new state out of the western portion of Florida started to really make the news. The teacher thought that if this bill somehow passed in Florida, and passed in D.C., then the Electoral College would be even more stacked, in her words, than it already was. Stacked against what, we didn't know.

People wouldn't take that, she said. People would fight.

Then somebody in the back row farted but no one knew who, and accusations and eventually chairs were thrown and the period ended and we all went on to gym.

Talking about civil war wasn't anything new. I'd been hearing that shit ever since I was little. Come election time everybody acts like their dog's just died or like all the dead beloved dogs have risen up from their backyard graves and howled.

Big deal.

For homework that weekend we were supposed to look up articles about how states get made and ask the people in our lives what they'd do in a civil war–type situation. The teacher had showed us clips of little protests happening in Miami, in Orlando, on the statehouse steps in Tallahassee. I knew I'd originated there, in Florida, and my classmates went there on vacation, but none of those places meant a thing to me. Watching at the time, you might get the sense that both sides were primarily in it for fun. The One Florida people were up in the cities from the center of the state to the tip of the peninsula, and it wasn't like they were being invaded or forced to do anything, just asked to let go of a portion of the state they themselves called Lower Alabama or South Georgia or whatever. What did anyone really have to lose? People had said for years to just let whoever they didn't like have their own island, or space, or state: round them up, turn them loose, and watch them fail.

I didn't look up any goofy-ass articles. I had research of my own to do.

Lately, I'd gotten back into checking for updates in the massacre threads, watching clips of Krista's stuff in secret and studying her face while she had a chain fight on-screen with a futuristic biker girl or was pulled into a frothing bloody sea by a demonic shark, to see if my own face shone through. What I hadn't done was search for my uncle Rodney, at least not since I was little. Back then about all I'd managed to track down was some high school running stats—no presence on social media, zero images. I mean, I was a nine-year-old, not the FBI, so he might've been posting somewhere, but it sure seemed like this Rodney didn't want to be found and, I guessed, he didn't want to find me, so I'd given up, until now.

It was the Friday evening before the Dakotas' eighteenth birthday and I was up in my room with my phone in my hands going, Holyshitholyshitholyshit, because Rodney Woolsack still wasn't on social—but he was on DU3L. This time when I'd googled him the top results were all from the gunfighting app, every link taking me to a page that said it'd work better if I just downloaded DU3L in the app store. I started kind of vibrating on the bedspread while the loading arrow spun. Sat up and tried deep breathing. Got close to the screen, eyes wide with awe as his profile came up.

Rodney Woolsack was ranked twelfth in handguns in the Northwest Florida region. Here were his gunfights going back a year and a half. How many he'd shot. How many he'd been shot by. His sidearm of choice. His sponsors. A quick interview he must've filmed himself. Finally, his upcoming appearances and events, the next of which was the Crescent City Gundown the following Saturday.

I said to myself, You gotta be fucking kidding.

I'd seen gunfights from DU3L before, thanks to Big Mike and the Dakotas and my own curiosity. Just highlights, though.

I didn't do the livestreams or watch training videos or gear reviews. Still, I must admit it had a certain appeal. I don't know if the ads are right when they say gunfighting brought peace and safety to a dangerous and unpredictable world, but I was glad there was something for mass shooter types to do other than bust into classrooms or wherever and blast random people like me. Now they could put themselves on DU3L and get the kind of antiheroic ending their hearts desired, or the thrill of inflicting themselves on someone else via bullet.

That night I made a fan profile and watched as many of Rodney's gunfights as I could. The more I saw him draw and fire, his opponents stagger, clutching wounds until the medic came to carry them off or drop clean-shot to the ground, saw him take his share of lead too, always coming back for more, the more a lump climbed up my throat and hung there diamond hard, and I got to thinking about how in a matter of days he'd be just down the road and his profile page had a message button I could just click and say, what exactly? If he'd wanted to find me he'd had the better part of thirteen years, and besides, what did I need another violent macho lunatic in my life for? I had plenty of them at home.

I was feeling all wound up and confused, so I went downstairs, where the Dakotas and their dad were on the living room couch watching something on one of their phones. The Dakotas sat on either side of Big Mike and they were all three hunched over, staring intently. I hung behind the couch and tried to glimpse what was happening on the screen.

The camera was on a dirt track that looped a grassy infield filled with people turning in the direction of a cloud of dust and smoke. None other than Rep. Troy Yarbrough gunning around the bend in an All-Terrain Apparel Bombardment Vehicle with toothy black wheels and a custom-mounted T-shirt Gatling gun and integrated trigger system. Coated in red and white, with #BestFlorida emblazoned on its roll bars and the logo of the red wolf prowling across the hood, the vehicle churned a stream of dirt behind it like bilge as Troy made toward the stage in a jackknife drift, firing T-shirts into the crowd. I watched hands shoot up, grabbing for the bundled shirts, scrums breaking out all around him. Men tugging off their jackets, guts wagging as they tore the bands from the fired shirts and tugged them on. The red wolf there too, on the shirts, loping midstride. Another version of it hanging at the bottom corner of the screen.

I realized I'd been seeing that wolf around on bumpers and hats without knowing what it meant. I'd assumed it was some gun or hunting shit.

Rep. Yarbrough got down and climbed onstage and was given a mic, and he began to speak and point. His sleeves were rolled in a Marine Corps tuck, and from the tips of his fingers to his eye sockets he was nothing but muscle and bone. Presently, he was joined onstage by a woman in a blush business suit with jagged spray-held hair the color of dried blood, leading on a thin leather leash an actual living red wolf. The Yarbroughs, husband and wife, cared so deeply about West Florida and its

environment that they'd put their own money into research-
ing and developing a hybrid strain of these creatures, with an
aim to reintroduce packs across the Gulf Coast.

The crowd roared and the wolf shrank back and sat at
the woman's feet as Rep. Yarbrough gave her a one-arm hug
and then began to speak. You could see the sinews fluttering
in his cheeks, if you could call them that. The man looked
flayed.

"That's sick," I said.

All three of them turned.

"Sick like good?" said Dakota James.

"Like he looks gross," I said. "Like he's super skinny."

"Dude's fricking ripped's what he is," said Big Mike.

"Vascular," said Dakota Blake.

"Striated," said his brother.

I said, Speaking of which, and told them about my homework, asked them what they'd do in a civil war. Instead of
answering, Big Mike turned back around and hit play on the
video, and they all three resumed watching. I asked again, for
real, and the Dakotas hooked their elbows over the back of
the couch and asked me what I'd do.

I said I guessed I'd probably fight and they said bullshit
I would.

So I asked what they thought I'd do, then, and the brothers looked at each other for a second and said I'd fill my pants
immediately. Dakota James broke into a freestyle built around
the end rhyme of poo and you.

"Savage," said Big Mike, his voice weighted with approval. Anyway, he added, it wouldn't be much of a fight because whoever was on the other side would be such beta-ass pussies that the war couldn't last too long.

He wasn't looking at me but I could feel his glare burning through the wrinkled back of his head. I worked on that diamond in my throat and left Big Mike and the boys downstairs. We had no idea what was coming, none of us.

Not a fucking clue.

CHAPTER TWO

THE BIG GUNDOWN

The night of the Dakotas' birthday we were having a crawfish boil and the cul-de-sac was swarmed with friends and neighbors and Big Mike's baseball buddies from high school and their kids in golf carts kitted out to look like characters from games. From my room on the second floor I could see the driveways and the turnaround filled with muscle cars and lifted trucks of all makes ranked down the street, wheel rims done in Devil's Dust, body paint jobs in Stinger Yellow and Maximum Steel. From their rear windows stared long-toothed skulls, piled bones, abstracted cameras, and, on their tailgates, hashtags for their followers and messages to those whose lanes they were blocking or in whose faces they were rolling coal.

My plan was to stay in my room until such time as I could sneak downstairs and peel a few pounds of crawfish in peace, but around eight p.m. I had to fill my Bubba keg. Most of the partygoers were out back playing cornhole or gathered around the roaring propane burners and the pots of roiling hell-red water, arguing about whether to dust the crawfish afterwards. I hated most of those motherfuckers but there's few things I love more than my fingertips working meat and fat from chitin and the sting of cayenne and salt on a hangnail and the smell of boil poured out into St. Augustine grass when it's all over. Wouldn't get to smell it that night, though.

I dodged a couple of neighborhood dads and some of the Dakotas' friends lined up for the bathroom and went into the kitchen with my Bubba. Miss Tina was in there at the counter, shucking corn for the boil. She was Big Mike's mom, but he didn't call her Mama and the Dakotas didn't call her Mimi or Maman or Meemaw or whatever. Miss Tina would tell you she did not survive Hurricane This and That to be called anything other than what she goddamn wanted. She lived on the lakefront in a condo on fifteen-foot stilts, but she was the reason our house wasn't a total disaster. When she wasn't picking up after us she was flipping tires and whipping ropes at CrossFit. She had close-set eyes and a leonine look, and she was snatching the silk off the corncobs and snapping them like they were the necks of tiny enemies.

I opened the freezer and was scooping fat thonks of ice straight into my Bubba when I noticed, there on the center rack, a plate with four loose hot dogs sitting on it. I stood there for a minute, blinking, fog swirling in my face, trying to make sense of what I saw.

"Shut that door," Miss Tina said. "You're letting the cold out."

So I shut that freezer door and filled my Bubba from the water thing, was about to head upstairs, but those dogs still preyed upon my mind.

I opened the door again and looked closer.

The plate was balanced on a pack of last year's deer sausage and it had to have been there since at least that morning because when I poked them the dogs were rock hard. These weren't long thin Nathan's, either, but plump girthy Ball Park franks, looking like they were about to split and they hadn't even hit the grill yet.

That wasn't where they were going, though. If those franks were destined for the boiling pot or the grill tonight they wouldn't be in the freezer, and if they were getting saved to be cooked later, they'd still be in their pack all stuck together in a harmless block. No, they were here and frozen individually because they were intended to go up somebody's ass.

Mine, namely, in the Dakotas' enactment of a then-viral challenge called the Chilly Dog. The challenge being to hold down whoever you're doing it to for long enough to get it all on video, I guess. I hadn't seen the videos but I'd heard the brothers watch them lately, filming their reactions, and at that moment I knew what was coming, the way you know somebody's watching you even though you can't see them yet. And if the Dakotas got ahold of me tonight there'd be who knows how many people watching.

I opened the door again and stared at the franks through the freezer mist.

Miss Tina gave a corncob a vicious crack. "I said, shut the doggone door."

I let go of the handle and the door swung shut.

"Finally," she said and went back to her work. Miss Tina was the reason there was even a clean plate to put hot dogs on, and probably had bought them too, though I doubt she knew what for. When I was little the Dakotas had used to do normal shit like hold me down and drip loogies in my face or blast a can of bear spray in my room and hold the door shut, but since their mom died they'd been edging more and more towards darkness. Still, there was a part of me that couldn't believe my adopted brothers had me slated for something like the Chilly. That's the problem: if you don't believe past the limits of what you think is possible, what you think the people around you are capable of, you're gonna live a life of shock and sorrow.

On my way back to my room I passed the bathroom line again and in it were two dads from the sac, talking football, and behind them a handful of girls, only one of whom I knew. Ink-haired and cowboy-booted Lacy Ardoin, who, a few months back, for the price of a single sad desiccated nug rejuvenated by the freshness packet taken from a thing of beef jerky, had been induced by the Dakotas to sneak into my bedroom, get up in my sheets and pretend to be some menacing yet sexual creature, growling and snarling while she mimed making out with me with oven-mitt hands. I'd screamed and suddenly there were phone lights in my face and everyone was whooping. I don't know what she was trying to be. Maybe the demon girl come back to get me.

The other girls in line were reading their phones but Lacy had her arms folded, staring at the carpet at her feet, while the dads in front of her talked loudly about how the Tigers, who, they both agreed, in the previous season had raped their opponents utterly, were at risk next season of getting raped themselves, raped on replay by SEC officials, raped in the ass by a resurgent Texas A&M offense, raped sideways by a bruising early schedule, prison-raped for their smallness in the trenches, specific players raped in the open field due to their inability to wrap up, for which they'd surely be verbally raped by the media the next day.

I was on the stairs, about to leave this conversation mercifully behind, when Lacy looked up from the ground and caught me in her eyes. Neither the dads nor the girls behind her noticed, and for a second there we shared what I thought was a look of mutual understanding, horror, entrapment, sadness. Like maybe she'd slip away later and come up to me with keys in her hand and say she was sorry about before and it was time we got the hell out of here.

Instead, Lacy jabbed her chin at me and said, "I bet you'd like that shit, wouldn't you?"

I turned on my heel and went back to the kitchen.

"You still here?" Miss Tina said, not turning from her work.

I took a sip from my Bubba and set it in the sink and went to the freezer and took the plate of hot dogs out.

I left Miss Tina there, still cracking cobs, and went out through the laundry room to the garage with the plate in my hand. When I went to dump the dogs into the big trash can, the condensation on the ceramic lip made the whole plate slip from my fingers and fall into the can. I stood there for a minute, holding the lid, weighing whether I was gonna stick my arm down there into the nasty dark to retrieve the plate, like it mattered.

The garage was crammed with tools and abandoned projects and vehicles—including the go-kart that melted my hand—all the things from when we'd been more like a family, immured behind rows of inventory, the stock Miss Tina sold on consignment and couldn't fit in her condo, leggings and freeze-dried food, and, most recently, pendants containing trace amounts of the authenticated blood of Christ reconstituted with pure Israeli water some preacher had blessed. A week or two after she stowed them here I snuck out with a box cutter and got one of the pendants and broke it open on Big Mike's workbench. I dipped my finger in the papercut's worth of dark glimmery goo and touched it to my tongue. It tasted like a Tiger's Blood sno-ball. Like the sweet blood of heaven.

I let the lid fall and stepped back, considering my position. Outside, the party was kicking into gear, and I heard the laughter and engines and the crackle-pop of Black Cats or small arms fire.

On one hand, throwing the dogs into the trash might've solved my immediate problem, but it couldn't solve the ongoing problem of what was going to happen to me here in the future. Like people kept saying about the coast: The era of short-term solutions was over. It was time to prep and plan for a future filled with absolute disaster.

Or maybe it was time to retreat.

I got out my phone and clicked DU3L and pulled up Rodney Woolsack's profile. I spread his pic big with my fingers and studied his face, as if closer inspection would help me make up my mind.

He wasn't what I'd been expecting, that's for sure.

The thing about gunfighter profile pics is they're always trying to look hard, staring bullets like the camera just said they had the little bittiest dicks west of the Mississippi. Rodney wasn't angry in his picture, though, more like he was profoundly sad about having to shoot you, asking why you'd brought yourself to this point of no return. His eyes, like my eyes, wide and searching for a reason not to do the only thing left. But the smile that curled the curled the corner of his mouth said maybe he was sad about how much he was going to enjoy this.

I took a breath and let the pic get small and messaged him before I lost my nerve.

About ten minutes later, I was upstairs shaking out my backpack so the floor was littered with folders and textbooks and those handouts that get wadded up and live compressed at the bottoms of backpacks for years, because no matter what, even if this guy, my flesh and blood, ignored me, I'd decided I was leaving here for good.

My phone shook and I did, too, when I read his message back.

Hold tight, he said. We're coming.

He must've torn out of New Orleans and redlined across the Causeway because it wasn't forty-five minutes before there was a knock at my door and Miss Tina's voice saying some people were downstairs looking for me. I hadn't even packed my backpack all the way but I slung it on anyhow and came out.

"I don't know what the hell you did," Miss Tina said, "but these two look like they about to haul you off to boot camp."

I shrugged and followed her downstairs, past the bathroom line and through the kitchen and the people playing quarters at the table where I'd done my homework, eaten breakfast, back when Amber was alive. My life here fading already.

When we came to the front door, I could hear the Dakotas somewhere behind us in the house or close by, calling each other bitch-ass niggas at the top of their lungs, one asking the other what he was gonna do. They'd fought before, plenty of times. They were brothers. But this fight sounded like they'd drawn blood, pulled the scab off some old wound between them. A girl screamed for them to *stahp it*, like girls who watch guys fight do. I felt bad for them, the girls, for all of us who aren't interested in watching people beat the shit out of each other and have to be there anyway, but I didn't wait or turn. I was going out.

Before I could open the door, Miss Tina grabbed the knob and stood there beside me, holding it open.

There on the porch was Rodney, looking older in person than seemed possible. I don't mean the sag to his cheeks or his puffed-up eyes that I'd later learn meant he'd been drinking, but the depth of the lines that time had carved into his face. They say everybody looks old as shit to you when you're young, but this was different. A desert of a face. His hair was long and pale blonde and swept back down his neck, and his eyes were lizard green. He was wearing a loose blue pocket tee and faded jeans and an automatic pistol on his hip. I didn't know a damn thing about holsters then, but I knew I'd never seen one like this. A black mechanism hanging from his belt that left much of the gun exposed, slide and frame gleaming in the porchlight. The right breast of his shirt bore a stitched profile of a bird of prey that might've been a bald eagle, but for the black mask wrapped around its eyes. Behind him and a half head taller stood a Black woman in a green polo with the logo of the Santa Rosa County Sheriff's Department on it. Like him, she wore a pistol on her waist, except her belt had pockets and pouches, and her holster was the regular kind. Her hair was cropped close and she was smiling at me like I was a stressed-out kenneled dog.

"Well?" Miss Tina said, gripping the doorknob like any second now she'd slam it shut.

I watched Rodney reach out all casual and lean against the door with his forearm, his left hand dangling. Slim fingers and a gold signet ring inset with a pair of Eyes of Texas diamonds and stamped with the words **LET'S RODEO**.

"Rally," he said to me, "you can come on out now."

His arms were laced with what appeared to be tattoos but were in fact scars, long ones that seemed to crackle at their edges and shorter white elliptical ones about the width of the blade of a boning knife. Even if you didn't know him for a gunman, anyone could read the story those scars told, see the speed coiled there in his wrists, the way he looked at you, sizing your next move.

"Rally?" he said again. "You ready?"

Nobody had called me by my name since school let out on Friday, so I blinked and stammered like a dumbass and almost looked back over my shoulder like whoever Rally was would be there.

Then I stepped down onto the porch.

"Now wait one goddamn second," Miss Tina said.

The Black woman held up a hand. "This'll only take a minute, ma'am."

"Don't you ma'am me, honey," Miss Tina said. "I'm not letting this boy come out with people I don't know. You think I'm crazy?"

"Ma'am—" Rodney said.

"You think I'm stupid?"

"Yes," the Black woman said, "but that's beside the point."

"You what?" said Miss Tina.

"I do," she said. "But the point is this young man's gonna come down and talk with us. Or are we having a problem?"

Miss Tina said nothing.

"Are we?" The woman was still smiling, giving a customer service voice, but you could see she wanted to get this over with before she had to do something she'd regret.

"Claudia," Rodney said, and she cut her eyes at him like this was all his goddamn fault, which I suppose it was. I saw the connection strung between Claudia and Rodney, swinging there like a power line in a storm, and I was a squirrel mesmerized by that transmitted energy. I didn't fully comprehend it, but also, for reasons beyond my comprehension, I wanted to race up and down that connection even though one good strong surge would blast me into a cloud of fur and yellow teeth.

Before Claudia could say whatever she was planning on saying next, Miss Tina slammed the door and left us out there on the porch. You could hear her storming through the house, shouting Big Mike's name. Rodney and I were staring at each other. He grinned, smoothed a lock of hair behind his ear, and I couldn't help but grin back.

"Well," Claudia said, "what're we waiting for?"

Down in the front yard a bloody-faced Dakota James was sitting cross-legged on the curb being tended to by Lacy and another girl who were dabbing their shirttails at his split lip, shining phone lights at his busted head. We were almost to the road when Dakota Blake rushed out from the back and stood over his three-minutes-younger brother, flexing, taunting, asking what the fuck he was gonna do now.

More people came spilling out of the backyard. A crowd gathering. Phones out.

"Excuse us," Rodney said, like he was angling his buggy around a jam in the grocery store. He put a hand to the oldest Dakota's shoulder and moved him aside, and Dakota Blake looked at me and said, "Murderbaby, what the fuck?"

I didn't answer and we went on down the driveway—Rodney, me with my backpack on, and Claudia—progress which both Dakotas marked now with slackened jaws and the pure silent astonishment of those who will never grasp what the fuck is happening, because they've spent their whole lives believing they already know.

We'd passed through a maze of chest-high tailgates, squeezed between chrome bumpers, made it finally to the turnaround of the cul-de-sac, the open street a straight shot ahead, when from the car-crammed driveways of the abutting houses came men in khaki shorts and athletic wear strapped with tactical equipment, as if at some signal they'd been summoned from their dens. Behind us the Dakotas were shouting now, and I turned to see Big Mike at the head of a crowd and armed with his AR-15, though of course he'd never call it that.

The rifle was his own build, ordered piece by piece from various dealers, modded for automatic fire, a drum mag hanging like a bubble gut from the stock. If he started shooting now it'd be a minute or two before he ran out. The driveway men were carrying too, and they strode down to where the tongues of concrete met the loop of the sac.

"I knew it," Claudia muttered. "I knew this shit down to the bone."

We'd stopped in the bull's-eye center of the turnaround. The driveway dads were circling us, racking their slides, talking shit. Hey, baby. Where you going? I didn't know whether they meant me or Claudia, because when these men did talk to me, it was in the same tone they'd use to address, say, a cart girl on the course.

Rodney's eyes were on the circling men but he said sorry to Claudia, and then he asked me, "You got any books in that backpack?"

I went, Uh-huh.

"Good," Rodney said. "Now put your backpack on so it covers your chest."

I felt us turning, like Rodney's and Claudia's eyes were spinning us along, merry-go-round-style, as they glanced from mark to mark and I adjusted my straps. Rodney eased down into his stance, knees flexed like he was fixing to surf. The driveway dads had stopped and stood now like skewed cardinal points, confident, with their homes and vehicles hulked behind them like giants brought to heel. Big Mike shouldered his machine gun and barked the start of an order he'd never finish.

They should've known better.

You don't fuck with a pistoleer.

The air around me exploded. Partygoers ducked and scattered and I saw Big Mike drop his weapon and follow it to the ground, cheeks ballooned, clutching his throat, a good portion of the top of his head blown off. I gaped, frozen for a second. Unable to believe the man was dead even though he was seeping all over the blacktop. The world as I'd known it was over and the shooting hadn't even stopped. The noise of it all about threw me down and I was the crouched, panicked hub in this wheel of death between Rodney with his automatic canted, dropping dads so fast their heads made coconut whonks on the pavement, and Claudia, her shooting arm flexed at the elbow, absorbing the recoil, her other tucked behind her lower back in a pose I've never seen repeated as she tracked the retreating dads with her sight and sent them spinning into yards and curbsides. Shots plunked the sides of the surrounding vehicles, tore real holes into chassis decorated with bullet-hole decals. All their lives these folks had fronted trouble and here, at last, was the real thing.

When the shooting stopped there was a second where all you could hear were the cries of the wounded and the cavernous roar the gunfire left behind. I got to my feet and

Rodney and Claudia were still standing, flexing like characters in a side-scroller, reloaded and ready to move out.

Rodney's truck was up on the curb just at the edge of the retention pond, the chrome grille nuzzled up to one of the fake lampposts the neighborhood put at the ends of everybody's yards. Rodney got his keys out but Claudia snatched them up and brushed past him and got in and cranked the engine. Rodney opened the back door for me and then went around to the passenger side.

The truck backed off the curb and whipped around, Rodney leaning out the window.

"Come on, dude," he said and clapped the door. "The Governor's waiting."

"I can't believe this," Claudia said. "Come *on*."

I wanted to say, The what? but I got inside and shut the door and we pulled away from everything I knew.

I kept it together really well for the time it took us to get down Causeway Boulevard, heading for Highway 22, on past the shopping centers and Tiffany Lanes, the bowling alley where Amber would take me to play the old Virtua Fighter and Soulcalibur while she did key bumps in the bathroom. I kept it together while Claudia got what she had to get out of her system, in a low dumb imitation of Rodney's voice, talking about, "Calls me out of nowhere like, 'Come on, babe, lemme take you to New Orleans. Just a tournament. I might die but

you'll love it, trust me. We'll rent a place uptown. Go to the
Maple Leaf, catch a show. Get you some barbecued shrimp.
Oh, by the way, I gotta go get some other bitch's kid real quick.
Have a shootout. No biggie.'"

Rodney didn't say a word, and I kept it together pretty
well as we made our way through the drivers swerving
their way back from New Orleans, until Claudia asked me
something.

"So," she said, "what'd they call you back there?"

"Who?"

"That boy with the busted head."

When I explained my nickname, Claudia said, "Oh," like
she was sorry.

"Shit, man," Rodney said. "That's fucked."

"It's OK," I said, suddenly on the verge of loud and messy
tears.

"That's right," Claudia said as she steered us on towards
the interstate. "We're gonna get you out of here and it's gonna
be OK, and when we get home"—she turned to Rodney—"you
and me are through."

At that point I wasn't keeping it together too well at all.

I tried to act like I wasn't crying, but Rodney heard me
and leaned around, going, "Whoa, whoa, whoa. What's wrong?"

"I'm sorry," I said, looking up through my fingers.

"Hey," he said, "it's not your fault." He bobbed his head
at Claudia like, See what you did? Then he said to me, "Look,
they didn't want to get shot, their asses shouldn't have—"

"No," I said. "I'm sorry . . . for everything."

Claudia looked at me in the mirror, asked me what in god's name was I sorry for. But Rodney knew what I meant. I wanted him to know I was sorry for what my mom and them had done.

At first he shrank a little behind the headrest, then he turned all the way back, so much that I thought he'd block Claudia's view and we'd smack into the taillights we were heading for at the intersection up ahead.

"Baby," he said, "you got nothing to be sorry for. You hear?"

All I could do was nod, sniff, tuck my chin to my chest and just get the rest of it out. We went on, and after a while Rodney reached for Claudia but she jerked her shoulder away and he slumped back into his seat.

Claudia eased us into the right-hand lane and up the looping on-ramp and we joined the nighttime traffic on I-12, an eighty-mile run of road stretched like a rope of spittle between Slidell and Baton Rouge in the jaws of I-10. It was awkward as hell in there, so I took out my phone. I don't think I'd ever had more than five notifications on my home screen before, but now the things were stacked so that I spent a good long while just swiping them away. I went to my settings and turned off tracking and started thinking maybe it'd be better if I just rolled the window down and tossed it out. Was just about to ask them in the front what they thought, when Rodney started making *ooh* noises and tapping his window for us to look at the shoulder ahead.

I saw the blur of trees and a blue road sign that I couldn't make out.

"There you go," he said admiringly.

Claudia was shaking her head, so I figured this was something between them, part of the fight I'd wandered into, until Rodney half turned and asked me, "You saw that sign, right?"

Claudia was soft-singing Ace of Base, which made me laugh, which felt good.

"I didn't see it," I said.

"West Florida Republic Parkway, motherfucker," Rodney said.

"That's what the sign said," Claudia explained. "He told me about it too."

"Yeah, but . . ." Rodney turned even more, to get a good look at me. "You know about that, right? I mean, y'all gotta drive on this road, like, every day."

I said, "I guess I never saw it? For sure nobody ever told me." Which was true. I had ridden this road more times than I could count, and I'd never had anybody point me out any signs, much less been inclined to look. "Is it just the one?"

"No, it's not just the one," he said. "Those signs have been on this road since before my ass was born."

"Really?" I said. "I thought it was, like, a new thing."

"Hundreds of years."

"The road?"

"West Florida," he said.

I said, "Like that guy Troy whatever?"

"Troy Yarbrough," Claudia said.

"The hell with him," Rodney said. "Guy's a prick."

We rode on in silence for a minute as the rain began to spit and pitter on the windshield. I told him about the teacher and the homework, and he told me how West Florida was a crown of crystal sand on the head of the gulf, unbroken. Rodney was breathless, excited, and while he told me all this stuff Claudia kept cutting her eyes at him and, in the mirror, at me, like to see if I was buying it because she damn sure wasn't. Anyway, the way he told it, West Florida had been taken over by one kingdom after another, colonized, contested, and split and subdivided so many times over the years that by the turn of the nineteenth century, when our however-many-times-great-grandfather, Angel Woolsack, and his adoptive brothers arrived here as tenants to run a store owned by Ohio's first U.S. senator, he didn't much care what country claimed to own the land. After all, the United States itself was a brand-new thing, and half the people who'd ended up down in West Florida, people like Angel Woolsack, had fled the new United States for being too official. Before he tried to be a storekeeper, our ancestor apparently had been a child preacher, ridden with the Reverend Devil John Murrell, prowled the banks of the Natchez Trace, and weighted dead men's bodies down with stones. Not exactly the storekeeper type. And neither were the rest of the cast-off Americans he ran into down here. They possessed, in the words of one historian, a hatred of taxation and other intrusive aspects of civil government, and a serious unwillingness to settle private disputes by any means other than violence.

Sound familiar?

I said, Yeah, it sounded like some people I knew.

And there were plenty of disputes to settle, he continued. You had your British loyalist royalist assholes who owned plantations and enslaved people and who'd stayed there even after Britain ceded West Florida to Spain, which was really more like Imperial France at that point, and there was this whole colonial shell game going on, but that's beside the point. These planters didn't like and damn sure didn't trust the trash people who were trying to run stores and do trapping, start businesses on loans they'd never pay back to people who owned other human beings outright, try and try in the hopes that they, too, could one day own human beings. The trash, like our ancestor, hated them back. So when the lawsuits and the mortgages spiraled into neighborhood vendettas, our ancestor and his crew of over-mortgaged rejects rose up and defied the Spanish curfews and rode masked and armed through Baton Rouge and planned to kidnap the governor, but reinforcements sent them fleeing to the backwoods home of Angel Woolsack, which he in turn fortified, until a group of planters in blackface—because that's how white people did it back then, they dressed up like whoever and said that's who'd done the crime—broke in and clubbed our ancestor and bound him and bore him down the Pearl River for delivery, ultimately, to Cuba. Saved by a detachment of American soldiers who just happened to be on the east bank of the river as they passed, he returned to West Florida and inaugurated a campaign of vengeance that lasted until he'd filled a jar up with human ears and every man who'd wronged him was deaf, dead, or had fled in terror. Not that Angel Woolsack was worth a shit either. After all that blood and righteous rage, what'd he end up doing for a living? He ended up being a slaver—a failure, like his revolt, like West Florida. Then about five years later the planters who'd wronged him had their own revolution against Spain, and this time, with more money and more help from the good old U.S.A., and no crazy-ass trash like Angel Woolsack to fuck it up, they won. The planters called it the Republic of West Florida.

"Shit never changes," Rodney said, when he came to the end of this part.

I asked him what he meant.

He said, "It was our idea and they took it. Fast-forward two hundred years and some other asshole's doing the same thing."

"But they won, right? So it worked out."

He snorted. "If you call that winning." And how could you, he went on, when their republic lasted about nine months before Uncle Sam scooped them up and parceled West Florida out, the natural boundaries ignored, this crown thrown down and smashed. It took another hundred years before Pawpaw brought it back.

I said for him to hold up.

"What?" he said. "You good?"

Claudia yawned and I said I was good but the guy who'd brought it back was his dad, right?

"Yep," Rodney said. "He was."

"So," I said, "You call your dad Pawpaw?"

Claudia snorted and clamped a laugh in her mouth. She might've thought I was kidding, but when Rodney's eyes flashed at me in the mirror he saw I was being serious.

"You're not the only person's had a weird-ass life, Rally," he said, and then he went on with his story.

RJ Woolsack didn't start out knowing or loving West Florida either. He'd grown up beautiful and ignorant in an age of prosperity and American preeminence, deep in the toe of Louisiana's boot, and himself wore Western-style pairs in elephant or buckskin so you could hear him coming from a good ways off, whether on tile or the institutional carpet of radio-station halls or the shell driveways of the properties he owned. He'd gone to school, first at LSU and then at the University of Texas at Austin, to avoid the draft and the enraged parents of the beehived girl he'd impregnated, and there, in the early seventies, he'd been spotted crossing Sixth Street by an advertising man. Within a year he had shot four campaigns for Nocona, two for Levi's, and ads for Kent cigarettes that ran in the middles of paperback books or in magazines dedicated to the bell-shaped boobs and teased hair of those days. He tried acting but wasn't as successful as his third wife Krista would be, with only a single credit to his name and, when his twenties ran out, he ended up with a trunkload of boots and the signet ring with the Eyes of Texas diamonds, now on Rodney's hand, and drove back to Louisiana, where he got into real estate and broadcasting.

By the time he was thirty-six, in the years of the Lincolns and the Armani suits, he had a daily talk show on WWL, and when Louisiana commenced to redden like a spanked ass in the late 1980s and his looks took a sharp fade, he switched mediums and politics and discovered both talk radio and patriotism. Discovered, finally, his lineage and West Florida. He'd been named by his mother, a girl of sixteen when she had him, for her two favorite actors, and he had no sense of his family's past because she'd tried fairly hard to outrun it.

But there West Florida was, waiting for him to sell to patriots who needed something to love when they hated their country with a passion. West Florida wasn't just an idea but a place, and he could sell it lot by lot, investment by investment.

It was a place to start again.

And he did, buying ad space in places like *Soldier of Fortune, Guns & Ammo, Gulf Coast Fisherman.* He cut call-in infomercials that ran on Pensacola public access for years even after his arrest, because he'd bought airtime in bulk. You'd see him there taking calls and talking about the coming state right before the show for followers of Yahweh Ben Yahweh, who sought the deaths of all members of the crazed and evil white race.

With the help of the believers he bought six acres of land off State Road 281 on the western shore of Garcon Point. The plan was to carve a contained community out of the land, with its own wells and power stations, schools and services. They got as far as cutting a couple of acres into lots and building on these lots roughly four complete plumbed and wired houses and as many shells of houses to come. On the choicest plot, overlooking Escambia Bay, RJ had begun to build himself an exact replica of the Louisiana governor's mansion in Baton Rouge, the one Huey Long had built, and on whose steps one night RJ, as a high school senior with a Dixie beer in his hand and about eight in his belly, had given an impromptu speech on his coming administration to the possums and the roaches scurrying in the steaming darkness.

Ten thousand square feet, fixed with marble and floating balconies.

Our home that never was.

Because neither Pawpaw RJ nor any member of our family ever got to live there, because the feds got him first and sent him to serve twelve years for fraud, money laundering, and conspiracy at Saufley Field, just off the naval air base in Pensacola. About ten miles from where his version of the state would've started. The property got bought by Emerald Coast Christian College, which was looking to set up a kind of retreat and satellite campus.

In '99, about a year into his sentence, RJ Woolsack escaped by up and walking off from his job tending the fairways of a golf course for fighter pilots, and fled into the open arms and homes of the last few true believers in West Florida, who hid him and succored him and with whose help Pawpaw eluded the authorities for almost two years before he was finally caught and sent to Texas.

Meanwhile, RJ's second daughter, the Governor's mother, a tall and vicious blonde called Alexis, had gotten herself into the minor leagues of the cocaine game and become charged as an accessory to attempted murder along with her half sister, his eldest daughter, Tara. Upon escaping these charges Alexis was taken in by Krista, until the whole family's various misdeeds bent back on them like a scorpion tail.

I listened to all of this and did think partly that Rodney and this whole world he'd spun might just be crazy as hell, but it felt good to be in it and in the shape of West Florida that was gathering in the darkness we were tearing through. You could almost see wild boys crouching in ambush with muskets and machetes, imaginary in their own lives, own times, ready to unleash themselves on the people who couldn't believe they were real.

We drove a while and I gathered myself some, started assembling the questions I wanted to ask. But I also felt queasy, and not just because I hadn't eaten since the night before. Whether I knew it or not I was coming to the edge, the one Amber wanted, in her best moments, to keep me away from. The more I think about it now, the more I think it wasn't some place I was headed for, but it must've been something she saw in me, something that'd been there all along. Because that's exactly what West Florida is, something in you. People call

West Florida a dream like that's supposed to be some kind of insult, like this place is no place at all but borderless, a vessel for us fucked-up people to pour our hopes and hang-ups into. But if this place that's not a place can be anything to anyone, then nothing can stop it from being real, and its borders can light up like neon in the sunset of any needful heart.

It was lighting in me then. I could feel it.

Claudia took the Lacombe exit and we left the interstate behind and took a state road into some old piney woods.

"Rodney?" I said.

"Yeah?"

"What'd you mean when you said 'the Governor'?"

Rodney grinned. Claudia shook her head.

"That's just what she is," he said.

Claudia turned back and added, "He's talking about your cousin Destiny. Or whoever's running around saying she's her. The Governor's what your Pawpaw called her."

I sat in stunned silence while she turned from the state road onto a gravel drive, into a cut in the woods.

"She's alive?" I said.

"Damn right she is," Rodney said. "And she wants to see you."

Claudia said she didn't know whether it was Destiny or not, but she didn't like it.

We went on another few minutes until we came to a kind of clearing at the edge of a ditch pond about a hundred yards across. A sewage lagoon scummed with a thick bubbling sheet of algae. Waiting there in the clearing beside the ditch pond was a bone-white pony car with a snarling hood scoop. When we pulled up I could see the shape of the driver through the window, like an animal living in the socket of a bleached-out skull.

Then its headlights came on and I couldn't see the driver anymore.

"All right, man," Rodney said. "Next step in the journey."

He popped his door and got out, but I stayed put. The more I looked around the more it looked like a great place to execute someone, and I felt like the dumbest piece of shit on earth to have been brought willingly to this end. I almost wanted to be back up in my room, hearing the Dakotas holding court below, and wake up in the morning to wade through the White Claw cans.

"You're good," Claudia said, but she didn't sound so sure.

Next thing I know, I'm gathering my bag and getting out, walking between them through the shell and the weeds to the pony car. I couldn't make out the model but its grille was black and its headlights round and its tires walled and polished so they shone in the moonlight. The passenger door swung open and Claudia made a small noise of surprise and Rodney gave me a half hug and said he'd see me in a little bit, see me at home.

I started over and took my backpack off and climbed into the night-cool leather seat with it in my lap and pulled the door shut and sat staring at the driver.

"My," she said. "Look how you've grown."

Her hair was paler than Rodney's and the longest I have ever seen, spilling over her collar and running past her waist to where I couldn't see. She wore a sleeveless turtleneck in black. Draped over the wheel, her left arm, encased in golden plate, crafted with wave forms and flowing floral shapes, hung there gleaming in the dome light.

Her mouth was thin and strange. She looked happy to see me.

The dome light ticked dim and went off.

"Do you know who I am?" the driver said.

"You're the Governor," I said.

CHAPTER THREE

THE ROAD TO HELL

The other side has the red wolf, which you can't hate despite its association—that animal didn't ask to be brought back from the dead, its genes shaken rudely awake—but the state beast of the real West Florida is the osprey, from the Latin *ossifrage*, the bone-breaker, for how hard this raptor hits the water when it dives claws-first for its dinner. Also called the fish hawk or the sea hawk, but not by anybody I know, the osprey, like West Florida's borders, can be found pretty much around the world. If there's water and fish, you'll find him there. The osprey gets his own meals live, brings them home to huge nests that house not only his family but families of other, smaller birds too. Because the osprey's strong enough to be nice to the little guys, let them live in his space, the Governor explained.

I gaped at her. Destiny in the flesh, or mostly. In the glow of the dash I thought I could make out faint gold pathways of circuitry showing through her temples, like baby veins.

The red wolf wasn't the only thing back from the dead.

I had about a million other questions, but instead I'd asked about one of the symbols etched into her arm among what I thought were sporting scenes and flowers and the like, and now all she wanted to talk about was this. I kept looking at her, my chest tight like I was in the presence of some massive celebrity, which I guess I was. At least to me.

Despite the osprey's penchant for housing the needy, it was originally chosen by Pawpaw and listeners of his radio show for being analogous to their whole anti-fed, anti-tax deal, because the hardworking, self-sufficient osprey often has his catch stolen by the sneaky and lazy bald eagle, who lives off others and dead stuff. Now, she said, we aren't so hung up on taxes or the federal government, because if you aren't a state in their books how can they tax you anyway?

"So, you don't want it to be a state?" I said.

"It doesn't have to be," she said. "Not in the traditional sense. We can be more . . . nimble."

"No taxes?"

"West Florida, our West Florida, is the osprey who helps his little pitiful neighbors, gives them a place to live, sustains them willingly."

"How are y'all gonna make people do that?"

She was quiet for a moment. "I'm not gonna make anyone do anything."

I stared at my feet. I hadn't packed extra socks and my toes were sweating, which is something that'd started happening in the past year.

"That includes you," she said, nodding to me.

While I sat there puzzling over it all, trying to figure which of my million questions to ask, the Governor got her phone and put a song on the radio. It began with gulls and breaking waves of synth before a drum machine took over and the singer started into a call-and-response with what sounded like a chorus of dudes. The official song of the state of West Florida under Destiny's future administration: "Go West" (1993).

I started nodding to the beat like I wasn't the slightest bit freaked. Truth was, it sounded like the OP from a nineties anime and that sort of tickled me.

"You know the Pet Shop Boys?" she said.

"Uh huh," I lied.

"Nice," she said, and the song went on and so did she, about synth pop and boystown, and meanwhile, I tried to listen to what the song was saying. About going our own way, leaving things behind, starting life new. Together.

"It's funny," I said, almost at ease for the first time since I'd gotten in the vehicle.

"Funny?" she said.

"Because we're going east."

The Governor looked at me for a solid minute without blinking. I wished she were looking at the road, for several reasons. But she kept looking.

"They're saying 'Go West,'" I said, "but we're really going east. It's funny."

Her gaze softened, like she realized I was an idiot, and she turned back to the road.

"Directions don't mean a thing, Rally," she said after a while, patting me on the head with her voice. "No matter what the signs say, we're going west."

I sat on that for a second, frozen there in the passenger seat with the shock of my name on her lips. That made twice tonight. Eventually, the song petered out and I thought that was the end of it but then the next track came, a funky bass lick followed closely by piano and blasting disco horns. When the chorus came on I realized it was the same song, just a different, older version. Where the Boys' had seemed sad, ironic, this was earnest and joyous. I wondered if maybe she had a whole playlist of versions of this song.

"Is this the Village People?" I said.

"*Very* good," the Governor said. "This is the original. The one Pawpaw played on his show."

The more I listened, the more I liked this version better, and I told the Governor as much. She seemed pleased enough, a wry smile growing on her near-lipless mouth. The song picked up and as it soared the Governor was drumming the steering wheel, her foot heavier and heavier on the gas, and I was scared as hell.

Then she started to sing.

Not at the top of her lungs but sort of low at first, urging me with her voice, and she leaned, looking at me, bobbing her head, mouthing the words like she wanted me to join in. I didn't know what to do with all my fear and nerves. But there she was, singing and singing, like there was nothing else to do in the world. Pretty soon the song took me in its disco-ball fist and yanked my nerves out by the roots and I was singing too.

As the mile markers whipped by and everything outside the cab blurred, I sang my heart out and so did she. Singing about how together we would love the beach, how we were going to where the sun shined bright in wintertime. We were going west. I'd been high and drunk before, and had eaten half a Xanax and a whole Klonopin, but I had never felt like this. Like all the compartments in my brain that were usually filled with small scared versions of myself talking about the worst things that could happen got sealed in one fell swoop and all those little frightened guys were silenced.

With this anthem roaring, both of us singing, we crossed Bayou Lacombe around one in the morning, the shoulders of the road all banked in fog, free and clear, until a state trooper's cruiser hidden at the foot of an overpass jerked out onto the road behind us with its lights and sirens going wild.

I looked at the Governor and she was staring in the mirror at the low dark Charger coming on through the swirl.

The Governor watched the cruiser in the rearview plow its menacing dazzle at us and kept going, so I ducked down in my seat while she put the cruiser through its paces. I didn't know if maybe there was an Amber Alert out for me or if they even did alerts for shitty preteen boys. I didn't know whether Claudia and Rodney had gone on ahead or if they were hanging back somewhere behind us like a shark, working through the shoals of late-night drivers. The Governor didn't seem to care.

I was preparing myself to be in the middle of another shootout, when something behind us in the back seat went *vreem*. I whipped around and saw lying lengthwise across the seat something like a dog, except this dog was armored and headless and its neck ended in a pair of vertical red lights. I heard the frictionless purr of servo motors. It was a quad, a gundog mech, and it went *vreem* again as it phased into its half stance and peered ahead.

"Down," the Governor said, meeting its optics in the mirror.

I sat frozen, not knowing whether this thing would home in on me as hostile and go all Chopping Mall, blast me with a laser, or what. I'd seen this kind of thing in videos, parades, but it was different when those red glowing eyes were looming just over your shoulder. If it had breath, I would've felt it on the back of my neck. Then the quad went *vreem* again and lowered itself back down into the seat.

"What *is* that?" I said.

"*That* is one of many. Troy Yarbrough's got a whole army of men. But who needs men?"

She smiled at me like, Present company excluded. I felt like a moron for not seeing the gundog in the back seat when I got in, but feeling like a moron wasn't anything new. This kind of fear was, though. The cruiser was still behind us, blasting light and noise, and I was about ready to pass out, when the Governor finally slowed and coasted us over to the shoulder and stopped beneath a billboard that displayed in cords of red neon the pulsing shape of an aborted fetus and some words about when life begins.

"It's OK," the Governor told me as she reached over my lap and undid the glove box. She took out an alligator-skin cardholder and closed the box, then sat back and rolled her window down and waited with her hands on the wheel for the trooper to come.

"You hungry?" the Governor asked. "Because I'm starved."

Too shook to speak, I watched the cruiser's door swing open and the trooper step out.

"When we'd pass through here on the way to Del Rio," she went on, "we'd always stop up the road here at Check-In Check-Out for po' boys."

The trooper came on, tall and narrow waisted, and as he approached he keyed the mic that hung from his left shoulder loop and spoke into it, striding on, backlit by his strobes. When he came to the window, he had to bend almost double to ask for her license and registration.

She handed the gator-skin cardholder to him and he took it but didn't stand. He just hung there, screwing his head to the side a little, trying not to stare at her arm. He was trying to keep his eyes narrow against the gleam of all that gold, just like I was trying not to look at him but couldn't help it. His shirt was pit-stained and unbuttoned at the neck. He took a flashlight from his duty belt and clicked it on and shone it into the cab, moving the beam from her to me.

He said, "Everybody doing all right in here?"

I smiled like, Yep, totally awesome time, and the Governor said, "Sure are."

He aimed his flashlight again, tracing the interior with the beam.

"Any weapons in the vehicle, ma'am?"

"Oh, absolutely," she said and went on to list her armaments and their locations until the trooper let out something between a whistle and a *tsk.*

"Work in a rough area?"

"You could say that."

"Which is?"

"Politics."

The trooper summoned up a grunty laugh and turned his light away. He flicked open the gator sheath and took out her license and shone his light on it so that the card glowed embryonic like the life-form on the billboard above, who watched this all unfold.

"Destiny Maetel," the trooper read. He glanced up at her and added, "Where we going this fast this late?"

"Home," she said.

The trooper consulted the license once more.

"Home as in Florida?"

"That's what they say."

"Not for long, though, huh?" the trooper said, flashing her another glance.

"What do you mean?" the Governor said.

"I mean if y'all have your way over there." He grinned, as if in awe at his skill with banter.

When the Governor spoke next her voice was crystal but you could see the wince ticking at the corner of her eye. "What makes you think we're with them?"

The trooper flipped the cardholder shut and tucked it under his armpit.

"Anyhow, you trying to make it there tonight?"

"If I have my way," the Governor said, "in about three and a half hours we'll be watching the sunrise on Pensacola Beach."

"Sunrise," the trooper said, testing the word like it was theory or prophecy. "And what brings you two to Louisiana?"

That wince again. Just for a fraction of a second. "We're visiting family."

The trooper bent down again, trying for some serious eye contact. "You and—?"

"Rally," I said, trying to smile at him. "I'm her nephew."

"Technically"—she turned to me with her forefinger up—"you're my cousin. But yes."

The trooper gripped his duty belt and asked us both to step out of the vehicle.

"Excuse me?" the Governor said.

"Let's just be calm, ma'am," he said. "We'll get this over with soon as possible."

Outside in the fog-damp, leaning on the hood of the Governor's ride, I figured this was the end. The Governor stood facing the trooper, her back to me, arms folded, so that you could see the glint of passing headlights, caught in her arm's gold plating, sent dancing across the trooper's forehead. She kept looking past the trooper towards the westbound lanes across the neutral ground, and the streaming traffic of eighteen-wheelers and the occasional car. I thought about Rodney and Claudia and where in the hell they were.

"Your nephew-cousin have any I.D.?" the trooper said. He had his thumbs hooped in his belt and the cardholder still up in his armpit.

"He's my cousin," she said.

"I see."

"He's thirteen years old."

The trooper nodded. "Which makes me wonder what he's doing riding around at one a.m. with you."

A flock of trucks roared past us, kicking up trash and gravel from the shoulder.

"Excuse me, sir," I cut in. "I'm just saying—I'd be glad to explain, if that's cool."

The Governor's lips skinned back from her teeth and she turned to me with a rictus smile that softened into compliance on its way back to the trooper.

"Excellent," he said and took the cardholder out of his pit, opened it and studied her license for a second, then snapped it shut and looked at me.

"What's her birthday?" he asked me.

"Her birthday?"

"Her birthday."

I stammered and before I could make myself form thoughts, much less words, the Governor leaned in front of me and spoke.

"Trooper," she said. "Do you know *your* aunt's birthday?"

"I might," the trooper said, and in the same breath tried to sexify his voice: "If she looked like you."

"Sir?" I said, sorry I'd ever opened my mouth. Sorry for everything.

His face darkened. "I'm waiting."

The Governor sighed and looked off to the westbound span. By the way she held herself I guess she was brainstorming the most efficient way to end this man's life, but it wouldn't come to that.

"January seventeenth, 1995," I said.

Her head snapped back at me and for a second she flat-out stared. I'm no freak for numbers but when you've read the articles so much, like I had, the facts and figures wear a

groove into your mind. Like, I knew how many times Rodney
had been stabbed, so that I could never look at him without
thinking *thirty-nine*.

I wouldn't see her that surprised again.

The trooper cocked his jaw. Snapped the cardholder shut
and told us to wait right there, he'd be back momentarily.

When I couldn't hear his boots scratching on the gravel
and he was at his cruiser door, I said to the Governor, "I didn't
know you were married."

She looked at me funny.

"Mrs. Maetel?" I said.

She snorted, turned away. "You don't know me at all."

"What's he like?" I asked, trying to be friendly.

"They're in tech."

Before I could press this line of questioning further, the
trooper returned and handed the Governor her cardholder
and stood unmistakably staring at her metalwork.

"Where'd you get that arm?" he said.

"Where'd you get yours?" she spat back.

"God," he said.

"Same."

Behind them, in the westbound lanes a couple hundred
yards off, a pair of headlights slowed and turned onto the neutral ground. I was the only one looking, and my ass tightened
at the sight of the headlights bumping over the grassy bank.

It was Rodney's truck and he cut across the eastbound
lanes and swung onto the shoulder just past the billboard

and sat facing oncoming traffic, facing us, headlights burning through the fog.

"Tell me, Trooper, do you know where we are right now?"

"Ma'am?" the trooper said. He looked to the truck and back.

The Governor went on, waving her forefinger. "If you're gonna say Louisiana, which I'm betting you were, just don't." She made a lip-buttoning gesture with her memory-alloy fingertips. "Because this, this is not Louisiana. OK?"

The trooper wasn't watching her anymore, not all the way. He was watching her and me and the truck ahead. "Ma'am," he said, eyes darting. He raised a hand to his mic but didn't key it, not that I could tell. The other hovered over his holster. He said "Ma'am" again, said he was gonna need to, um, but she didn't let him finish.

She pulled what looked like a business card out of the gator-skin sheath.

"Here," she said.

He took the card with his radio hand and you could see from the way he held it that the card was heavier than he'd expected. He hefted the card and rubbed a corner of it between his fingers like he was trying to see what it was made of. He looked up at her. He didn't seem like a cop anymore, just somebody who'd misjudged both the depth and the nature of the shit he'd gotten himself into.

I should know because I felt that look on my face too, for all that night and for many days to come. I'd pass a window or a mirror and that's what'd be looking back at me. The Governor, though, seemed like this was all going according to plan.

. "It's yours," she said. "Keep it."

The trooper's mic squawked but he ignored it and stood turning the card over in his hands. While he did, the Governor was telling him how where we were right now wasn't Louisiana, hadn't even been part of the Louisiana Purchase.

"If I have my way," she said, "this will be West Florida too."

She went on, giving him a history lesson. Me, I was too busy trying to see what was on the card to catch everything she said. Too busy also looking over my shoulder at Claudia and Rodney's ride parked up ahead, rumbling like a tank. I'd hear it again anyway, in about five minutes. Just like I'd get to see those cards so many times they might as well be stamped on my brain.

The cards she handed out were always quality, made out of the finest metals. Not like the ones I'd come to find the Yarbroughs would encourage local agencies in the panhandle to put on their websites as PDFs for people to print and fill out and carry. You'd run into all kinds of stocks and colors with those. But the Governor's cards of the first run, the official exclusives, were thin sheets of pale-blue alloy embossed with a diving osprey, ringed with stars, one for each of the counties and parishes of West Florida. The words declared the holder of this card an official citizen of the state of West Florida and entitled to all the rights and benefits accorded thereby.

"I don't know," the trooper said.

"Sure you do," the Governor said. "I bet you've known it deep down all your life. Maybe not exactly what or why, maybe just as a feeling. Just like you're out here on the lonely road watching all the wrongdoers go by and you get the sense that things are getting blurry at the edges, and no amount of blinking's gonna make it sharper and you're falling in place, reality and fantasy merging into a timeless dream.

"But now you have a name for it," the Governor said. "Now you know, and everything afterwards is going to make so much sense. And one day you're gonna look back in wonder at this moment when it all began."

Above us the fetus pulsed, and past the billboard Rodney's headlights burned through the fog and the dark. The trooper didn't speak again. Slipped the card into his breast pocket and started for his cruiser, going sort of sideways, watching us all, the way they say you should exit an encounter with a bear.

We waited there until the cruiser fishtailed into the road and made a U-turn over the neutral ground and headed westbound, away from us. Up ahead, Rodney's truck ground into drive and swept onto the road, leading the way east. The Governor smiled and went around to the driver's side and opened her door, and I did the same on mine.

"By the way," she said, "next time, maybe don't offer to help the cop."

"OK," I said.

Her voice softened, sensing my shame. "It's fine. I know your intentions were good." She leaned against the doorframe, took in the night and sighed. "But what's the road to hell paved with, right?"

"Do what now?"

"The road to hell," the Governor said, slowly, like I could finish it for her. "It's paved with . . . ?"

"I don't know," I said. "With skulls and shit?"

We hit I-10 and the traffic picked up as we got closer to the coast. Around Ocean Springs the fog broke and a rainstorm descended on the road, hemmed us in, smaller, closer than before. My stomach was aching hollow and I might've been more than a little out of it. But I didn't know if I'd ever get this chance again and so I turned to the Governor.

"Can I ask you something?"

The Governor thumbed at her phone and when the message sent, she looked up.

"Shoot."

I took a big breath. I still had my million questions, but this was the one that came.

"Did you kill my mom?"

The rainfall seethed against the windshield, so thick you could barely make out the road, the lights, the way forward. We passed cars pulled off on the shoulder, lights flashing.

"Yeah," she said. "I shot her in the side of the head in the garage. She was the last one."

The Governor tapped the brake and we slowed, crawling up to join a chain of blinking hazards that stretched on into the night. The morning. Whenever we were.

"You went to school with her," I said, cautiously, wanting to know more.

"We weren't what you'd call friends."

"But you knew her."

"Yeah," she said. "I knew Nessa."

The Governor told me how Nessa ran up on her one day in the bathroom at school. She'd been at the sink and Nessa came out of the stall behind her and stood there in the fog of her own stank, like she had something she needed to say, bad. The Governor thought she maybe wanted to fight, but Nessa said, You got a little brother?

I've got a little uncle, the Governor said. Two of 'em, actually. They go to Brown Barge Middle.

"My dad?" I said.

"Yeah," she said, sadly. "Next thing I knew the Avon lady who lived across the street from our house had backed her pink Escalade into Nessa's busted-ass Saturn." She looked at me. "She'd parked off to the side of the house and Kenan'd snuck her in."

"You didn't like her."

"I didn't like that she liked him." The Governor narrowed her eyes. "Your grandma, Krista, she's the one really hated that girl. Didn't want her boy laid up with some senior." She squinted ahead. "Those people you lived with back there didn't tell you all about her?"

"Yeah, but—"

"*But*," she said, and sort of let that sit in the air for a while. "I get it. You deserve to know. I mean, I didn't come all this way to get you and bring you home thinking you didn't deserve some answers. Anyway, your grandma absolutely hated Nessa Pace. Despised her. My mom hated her too. Said she was fast, which is funny coming from someone like her, but still."

"What about my dad? What was he like?"

"Rodney," she said, "can tell you more about him. We all grew up together, but it's different between brothers, you know?"

We'd come just about to a complete stop, the rain rushing down the windows like we were in a car wash, and she turned and studied me.

"Now," she said, "can I tell you something?"

"What?" I said.

The Governor smiled, face lit red from the hazards. "When I walked out of the house, all covered in blood, I went down the driveway and there was this car I didn't recognize parked at the curb. I remember standing there at the edge of the driveway, right where it met the road. I was staring at the water, in shock, and I heard this sound like a phone buzzing. *Buzz buzz. Buzz buzz.* So I go over and I look in and"—she caught her breath—"there you were. Crying your goddamn head off. All strapped into your seat, eyes tight, crying like hell. I touched the window and it shook. Like the whole thing was alive. That's what I remember. Just being amazed that anything could be alive. So I knocked out the driver's side window and then I left."

I'd never heard about the window in any of the reports, the forums. Maybe it was a lie, or maybe it was one of those things the cops kept secret so they could spring it on the true culprits.

"Where'd you go?"

"You wouldn't understand. Not yet. But I had to go. I don't know what I would've done if I'd stayed."

"Like what?"

"Like, once you start killing people, it's not something you can really turn off." She nosed the car onto the shoulder and peered into the rain. "I think I would've eaten you. Like a shark."

"So why didn't you?" I asked.

"What, eat you like a shark?" She drummed the steering wheel, thought about it awhile. "Well, for one, you're family."

It felt so good to hear her say, but that wasn't what I'd meant.

"I meant why'd you wait so long to come get me?"

The Governor was quiet for a long time. The traffic had started flowing and the phone was pinging with messages. She'd turn it over now and then, glance and swipe.

"Who says I waited?" she said.

"Bloody 98," the Governor said into the sunrise, like this was the best thing ever.

I didn't know if she was talking about a year or what.

I'd learn our state holidays for celebration and others for solemn remembrance. There were days still to come that would be remembered forever. But for the moment I was just slipping on the learning curve, like I was trying to run up a half-pipe.

We'd left the interstate and the rain behind, back under the Mobile River as the Governor gunned the engine and the concrete mouth of the George Wallace Tunnel spit us out like bullets aimed at the heart of West Florida. I'd been dozing in the passenger seat and even before I opened my eyes I could feel the sunlight blasting over me.

"What's that?" I said, meaning Bloody 98.

My skin was hot, paler than it would ever be again, and I was blinking like a mole. The Governor had slipped on a pair of shades with big mirrored lenses that came down over the tops of her cheekbones, and now she flicked a panel on the dash and took out a similar pair and handed them over.

"You're on it," the Governor said.

I sat up, neck cricked, and tried to see what she saw, but the road ahead didn't look any different from any of the other ones we'd taken to get here. It wasn't like the clouds ahead were raining gore down on the greasy blacktop. Mostly what I saw was the sun, orange and huge behind puffball clouds that caught and threw its glitter everywhere.

I did a sly little check of the back seat, to see if the gundog was still there. Sure enough it was, limbs tucked up and optics dim.

The official scenic highway of our state, Bloody Highway 98 runs from the contested portions west of the Perdido and along the coast for the length of the ten true panhandle counties. Through the zones of opportunity and commerce dotted with chain link–bordered cenotes of runoff rainwater and through the ruins of fun centers. The shoulders and embankments of the road are decorated with crosses and flowers and stuffed animals staring out through muddy eye beads, the site of countless wrecks caused by carelessness or rage or some unfortunate combination of the two.

Like our family and the state itself, Highway 98 is half beauty and half horror. You can't look around and not be stunned by the glorious gulf and its accompaniments. Like us, for years the highway made attempts to shake its violent and tragic reputation, with lights and speed limits, but the people of West Florida don't like limits.

"I'm going to drop you off at your new place, with Rodney," she said. "But first we've got to do something important."

We took the highway through Daphne and Foley and down to where miniature fighter jets flocked along the legs of bridges into the West Florida capital city of Pensacola. This had been the site of the old Spanish administration, with streets named for some of their generals such as Palafox, my favorite, who promised invaders "war right down to the knife." Though of course the capitol itself, the house of government, is wherever the Governor happens to be, for the government follows with and is inseparable from her, and we are lost without it, misdirected as hatchling sea turtles following somebody's floodlights.

On an algae-stained overpass we skirted the campus of Emerald Coast Christian College, which laid claim to five acres of lowland, the souls of eight thousand students, and the home of the Yarbroughs, Troy and Rachael Kingdom, whose family, the Tates, had founded this whole thing in 1978, starting out of a single office building.

It was the dream of its founders, Anson and June Tate, to provide a college-level education along the Christian tra-ditional approach—like they'd received at Bob Jones Bible College in the sixties—but on a scale that rivaled campuses where the more humanistic progressive educational approach was taken. They hoped to tempt students with amenities such as pools, field houses, bowling alleys, dining halls, movie the-aters, and whatever else would make boys and girls eager to come and train for a life of service to the Lord Jesus Christ, rather than for the radical political, sexual, and cultural baccha-nal rampant in those worldly institutions. They believed that the area of northwest Florida itself was ripe with enrollment potential and could attract students from around the country. But in order to do that, the Tates needed money, and the Tates, when they arrived in Pensacola with their five children and few belongings stashed in the back of a Ford Mustang II that had barely survived the drive from Oklahoma, didn't have enough. They'd bought a small building and its contents sight unseen on a loan financed by the sale of their house and business in Tulsa and come to Pensacola without strong connections to any local church community and only a vague affiliation with a constituency of churches across America. Without immediate fundraising prospects, despite the fact that they had bought half-page advertisements in Christian journals and bulletins nationwide advertising their school with its green-gleaming name and coconut palm–overhung logo, the Tates prayed and searched their souls and, more importantly, the lower floors of the building, where a pair of massive antique Linotypes hulked among moldering rolls of paper, all of which they now owned. Thus they were given the first of many answers to their prayers.

That fall, while her husband organized the college and hired faculty, June Tate sat with stacks of K–12 textbooks scrounged from dumpsters and donated by concerned parents, and painstakingly excised their more worldly contents. She rendered the remainder down to what she saw as the pertinent facts, reframed in harmony with God's truth in the various academic disciplines, created curricula, workbooks, benchmarks, an entire educational ecosystem to be populated, she dearly hoped, by the children of Christian parents nationwide who had been suffering their impressionable young to be trapped in secular schools five days a week, nine months a year. She worked steadily at this in tandem with the creation of ECCC's own academic pathways, while learning the arts of copyediting, typesetting, and the operation of the temperamental Linotypes, which she taught to her children, who became a fixture in the printing room and were called, by June, her printer's devils. She advertised her wares, published under the name Dolphin Books, to the growing homeschool movement almost entirely by word of mouth.

And she prayed more.

By the spring of 1986, when the first applications started to drift in, mostly from local families the Tates had made contact with but also a few from out of state, a miracle occurred. June sold out the initial print runs of every textbook and workbook she'd made, some of which were stamped with the breaching dolphin colophon of Dolphin Books, amended with a cross on its cetaceous flank years later, when the renamed ECCC Books dominated both the homeschool and Christian secondary educational textbook market. The money from those initial sales sowed the seed for the college's growth over the next three decades, with steadily increasing sales and strong enrollment figures, leading to burgeoning community partnerships with wealthy Christians. These families bought parcels of land around the Dolphin building and sold it to the Tates at a loss and then wrote off the loss on their taxes. The local tax assessor, Don Yarbrough, orchestrated the devaluation of an entire neighborhood off Palafox and waterfront lots spread around two counties, and conspired with the Tates to purchase the land that had been ours, the promised West Florida neighborhood on Garcon Point. Finally, under the leadership of Rachael Kingdom, the Tates' eldest daughter, who would come to inherit the main ownership of the college and its related enterprises following her marriage to none other than the tax assessor's son, Troy Yarbrough, in 2008 following the murder of the elder Tates while they were on a mission to Haiti, ECCC became what the promotional literature described as a state-of-the-art campus, whose gorgeously landscaped grounds—maintained by the college's own students of landscape architecture and golf course management, a fleet of suntanned Oakley'd boys zooming soundlessly in motorized carts along the manicured lanes, tending to the baize perfection of St. Augustine lawns and their fringes of monkey grass and the boughs of crepe myrtles that flowered famously in spring—reflected the orderly will of the Author of the universe.

"Rodney and Kenan's mom would send them there for summer camps, sometimes."

I tried to imagine them young, sitting cross-legged with a dozen other kids on some gigantic institutional carpet, as I'd done, men and women going among them, asking them if they were saved.

"Was Krista super Christian?"

"Sometimes," the Governor said, "when your man's in jail and your boys are seven or eight and your best friend is all fucked up on drugs, you get sucked into stuff like that."

"So y'all were in with them. The Yarbroughs."

"My mom didn't hang around that church stuff, so I didn't either, and your Grandma Krista shook it off too, after a while." She yawned, stretched. "But Rodney could tell you better.

Him and Kenan were the ones that caught the brunt of it. The Tate's daughter, Rachael Kingdom, she even babysat them for a while. Rodney went over to their house and all that."

We passed through East Hill and skirted the neighborhood where Grandma Krista had grown up, on the banks of Bayou Texar, a low narrow gash of water torn in the eastern portions of the capital, in the shadow of a phosphate plant that had left a plume of poison in the groundwater of the surrounding neighborhood before it was decommissioned the year she was born. Class-action notices in the mailbox in the early nineties ("Is your property in the ZONE?").

The Governor told me how, when my grandma was done with being a Hawaiian Tropic girl and straight-to-VHS bit player, when Pawpaw was in prison in Texas, Krista had taken a job at the tax assessor's office, worked for Don Yarbrough, who seemed like just a standard-issue ambitious local politician. Sure, maybe he pushed the staff hard, and maybe his son Troy was kind of weird and you'd hear about the trouble he was getting into at FSU, but when Hurricane Ivan had fucked up the house in Tiger Cove to the point that it was uninhabitable, Don Yarbrough was the kind of guy who'd lend his family's second beach house to you and yours.

Unluckily for Don, the people he'd been so generous to also happened to get themselves killed in spectacularly gory yet mysterious fashions, which threw a cloud of suspicion far and wide, in whose shade the public started to see potential conspiracies afoot. Affairs that needed to be covered up. Cover-ups gone wrong. So Don's ambitions ended in Escambia County, but he still had money amassed and a son to bankroll.

Daddy Don wouldn't live to see Troy's full and final climb, though. He died when Troy was still in law school of a heart attack that his son blamed not on arteries but on the state and local news. At his father's funeral he addressed these outlets and their reporters by name and used a quote from the movie *Tombstone* that pretty much said he'd be coming for them.

Midday we passed onto the lone standing temporary span of bridge that stretches over Pensacola Bay, running parallel to the ruins of several versions of the old Three-Mile Bridge, pontoon crews bobbing around the sheared blocks of busted concrete, spray-painting circles around exposed nerve endings of rebar, plans for work so that the next hurricane could knock them down again, coming onto Santa Rosa Island and the town of Gulf Breeze, where I'd spend the coming summer in a ranch house with Rodney just off 98, at the western edge of Butcherpen Cove. A little neighborhood wedged between the Publix shopping center and the national seashore that goes for three miles on either side of the highway. Three miles of undeveloped dune beach and mangrove root and saw palm and sea oak jungle and properties fronted with paddocks fenced with salt-worn hunks of drift, where horses stood in the sandy yards chewing at clumps of sweetgrass.

West Florida can live in any heart, but if West Florida has a heartland, then it's there.

We passed the turnoff and the road I'd soon travel so often that I'd come to know every chunk of blacktop and fallen limb and plastic bottle dip-stained amber. We went on without a word until the Governor sighted to our right the rainbow-finned sign pointing us to Pensacola Beach, an atomic-age version of a leaping sailfish, its dorsal fin a ray-gun blast of neon, gorgeous even morning-dim.

We got to the beach via yet another bridge. Everywhere here is bridged or causewayed, passages nested with granite riprap blackened occasionally with the burn spots from run-off cars, linking the chain of crystal barrier islands that necklace the panhandle. Disaffected locals and jealous inland types like to talk about how we have to barge in sand from elsewhere to shore up our beaches, and I have to ask where in the fuck does someone like that think sand comes from anyhow? I'll tell you: it comes from mountaintops and riverbeds and millions of years ago when it gritted the gums of dinosaurs—so I say it might as well come here from Texas sometimes on a barge.

At the tollgate, the Governor paid our way with an actual one-dollar bill, which the tollkeeper pinched at clumsily like it was a butterfly trying to flap away and almost dropped because he couldn't take his eyes from her arm.

"That thing for real?" he said, pointing to her arm.

"Real as real can be," the Governor said while her other hand drifted down to the gearshift and gripped the ball tight.

The tollkeeper had leaned out of his booth for a closer look.

"I sure didn't think that kind of thing was possible yet."

There was no one behind us and the bridge stretched empty on ahead. I searched the mirror for the Governor's eyes and watched her hand on the stick, thinking any minute she would draw a piece and splatter him, or up and crush his wattled neck in her metal fist going, "This real enough for you?"

Instead she spoke.

"A great American from the 1970s," she said, "had a motto: 'If it is possible, it has been done. If it is impossible . . . it will be done.'"

The tollkeeper leaned back into his booth and offered guesses as to who she was quoting, but she didn't tell him, and finally he pressed some unseen button that lifted the gate arm and off we went.

When we came off the bridge onto Beach Boulevard, at the split where the road branches into Via de Luna to the east and Fort Pickens to the west, the Governor turned us right and we headed for the fort. The sun was in our mirrors and we drove past a badly damaged Jimmy Buffett's Margaritaville Resort, stove-hulled boats caught in the rigging, and through the hotels and the houses and the unreconstructed ruins of hotels and houses, until these buildings thinned and disappeared altogether and the dunes rose up and loomed over the shoulders of the road.

In the distance, over the crests of the dunes, you could see the walls of Fort Pickens. Twenty-one and a half million bricks seamed with grass and sunburst lichen, walls that'd once held the Chiricahua Apache rebel Geronimo along with fifteen of his warriors and their families, set to hard labor in 1886. If we'd turned the other way, we would've passed the stretch of beach where the first white settlement on these shores was laid and occupied and obliterated by hurricanes about three hundred years prior to the warriors' internment.

I didn't know a bit of this but it was all getting baked into me, burnt there by the sun.

We drove deeper into the beach. Clouds of sand blew off the slopes of the dunes and drifted across the road like mist. The whitest sand you'll ever see. We parked on a deserted patch of shoulder, no vehicles ahead or behind that I could see. I opened the door to a different kind of heat than the one I'd known back when. Less sticky, more like if a witch or sorceress had trapped you in a diamond and set the diamond on the burner on the stove. I melted out of the seat and onto the shoulder, dripping around to the Governor's side, where she said for me to come on. I looked in the back at the quad dog, but he seemed fine, stretched across the seat. I followed her across the road until she stopped abruptly on the faded center stripe and turned and stood looking at something on the ground at my feet.

"Leave 'em by the car," she said.

"What?"

"Your tennis shoes," she said. "Leave 'em."

I didn't know about that. The heat of the road was baking through the bottoms of my sneaks and the air above the blacktop was squiggly. This was going to hurt, I knew, but it felt like a kind of test, for there she was, standing barefoot, towering and gleaming, and at the thought of disappointing her, my insides writhed like the air. So I went back and sat against the bumper and kicked my shoes off and toed off my socks and hurried after her on the outsides of my feet, across the road and into the dunes.

Ticking bugs in the rosemary bushes and squadrons of dragonflies moving all in one direction like they do. It was a path people had used, and though there wasn't anyone around, there were traces everywhere. Orphaned flip-flops. Crushed cans. A sign instructing us to obey the following rules and otherwise to have a sun-sational time. The sand burned but in a different way than the road, and it spoke in powdery squeaks.

We went down to the water and I stood in the surf, letting my feet cool. Baitfish shimmered by and a ray came up and fluttered its fins at me. After a while she had me sit in the sand in a patch of what should be our state flower—beach morning glory—but isn't. The Governor took a higher place just behind me and sat staring at the gulf, stone-still, like something charging up, power bar flickering.

Prior to this, thanks to trips to Orange Beach and Grand Isle, I associated the beach mostly with stings and burns and Big Mike getting into a fistfight at some bar or punching out the mirrors in the condo or the Dakotas cutting backflips at the hotel pool until one of them busted their head. All that kind of shit was probably happening on this same beach, or had happened the night before, or would happen in a matter of minutes, but you'd never know it then, we were so alone.

The gulf rolled at us, molten, in the sun. Ghost crabs peeked out of their holes and little birds with twiggy legs skittered by, leaving dino footprints in the wetpack. Pelicans and gulls swept over the water, shadowing mullet. I picked at the little white petals of the beach morning glory, squished them, smelled my fingers—nothing there.

The true state flower of West Florida, so I'd learn, is the gas station rose, found on lotto ticket countertops beside the buckets of miniature Chick-O-Sticks and the energy shots and those pralines nobody buys.

The next time I glanced back, I saw the Governor had turned her gaze from the gulf and was now looking hard at me. Her mirror shades like pools of mercury, and me up in the lenses, trembling.

"Turn around now," she said. "It's time."

I did turn and sat before her cross-legged, like any second I was going to receive instruction or a blessing. Likewise, I didn't know whether this was insane or awesome, which I guess you've got to expect when you're a storybook orphan rescued at last by your true family. In the end it was a little of both.

The wind was at the Governor's back and it took up her hair as she rose and spoke. "We've lost so much," she said. "Our inheritance stolen, our futures replaced by the half-cocked reboots of someone else's story." She paused. Took a breath. "But that won't always be the case."

I held my knees and rocked forward in the sand.

"Rally," she said, "I want you to close your eyes and feel the heat and listen."

I did and the Governor's image burned in a web of fire for an instant and then faded against my eyelids. Waves of cartoon lava warmth. The sudden chill of her fingertips on my forehead. Then she told me a story about her mother that went like this:

On the banks of the Mississippi, in Baton Rouge, West Florida is home to the oldest visible human structures on earth. When my mother knew them, they were called the Indian mounds, and children sledded down their slopes on sheets of cardboard and drunken car wrecks were consummated at their base. The mounds lay at the heart of LSU's campus, and in the fine weather she and others of her kind would go between classes with beach towels and lie atop them like sacrifices to the sun, sacred and immobile in their hip-cut suits.

One day a girl she'd never met before climbed up to where my mother lay and sat beside her, talking. She told me later the girl sat in front of the sun, so she couldn't see her clearly, wouldn't know her face, but her voice was frail and trembled as she spoke. The girl told my mother she was laying on something that had been built by a great and beautiful people whose works had been soaring spires of earth and bone and shell. Alexis listened, seeing in her mind the spot where she lay raised up to the clouds and ringed with jewels of sunlight. On the opposite slope, other sun-bathers who'd overheard were laughing.

"What happened to them?" Alexis said.

"Fucking aliens beamed their asses up," said a pledge on the eastern slope.

"I'm serious," Alexis said, and the laughter ceased and the only sounds were of people going to class and the cars streaming around them through the campus. The girl beside her leaned over and before Alexis could pull away had pressed something hard into her hand. A little milky crystal she would lose nine months later when the cops tore her car apart.

"Same thing that's going to happen to us," the girl said. "The water comes or the fire comes, the desperate people come or the wicked people come and suddenly everything you know is gone."

I opened my eyes without being told, and I was worried until she smiled.

"You're here now," the Governor said. "Where you were always meant to be. And the wicked people are here, too, wearing our own skin. Don't be scared. Your path has always been shadowed by violence and revenge and crazy-ass white people. Listen to the sun roaring, feel the radiation altering your cells, and know that soon this summer we will each be called forth and changed according to that power, into what we were always meant to be. Are you ready?"

I said I was, I would be, without saying so out loud.

"Good," she said. "Now get up."

I did that too and followed her in a daze back to the shoulder of the road, where Rodney was parked, leaning there against his truck, Claudia nowhere to be seen.

The Governor unlocked her car and I got my bag, lingered there for a moment, looking at the quad, which lay across the back seat and didn't seem to care I was there.

When I came around the tailgate I saw Rodney and the Governor embracing.

Him all drawn up like a crushed spider in her arms.

I didn't think the Governor would follow us to the house. I knew this was some kind of goodbye, but even as she let go of him there on the shoulder of the road between the dunes, and his face fell with the touch of her fingertips and he looked like he was about to squall, even then I believed I'd be seeing her again before long.

CHAPTER FOUR

WESTERN ROMANCE

Sometimes on those gunfight summer evenings, after he'd put his range hours in, Rodney would drive us out past the zoo and the Walmart, to a shell-and-gravel lot where a man was smoking mullet in an oil-drum rig hitched to the back of his Ram. The man had welded the smoker and trailer himself, he was always proud to say. Prior to this he'd worked transport for oil companies at the mouth of the Mississippi but had quit for his mental health. Every year, he said, he had to prove he could escape from the cabin of a sinking helicopter in under thirty seconds, and that was no way to live or die.

In the tailgate of his truck were two big white plastic coolers of the old style, not that Yeti bullshit, one filled with salted ice and Cokes and cans of Gulf Lite beer and the other with cleaned mullet and tubs of creamy smoked-fish dip. Rodney would buy a Gulf for himself and a Sunkist for me and enough tinfoil-wrapped sides of fish from the smoker and tubs of dip for us both.

He'd drink the beer and I the Sunkist on our ride back to the house. We'd go straight from the carport around through the banana plants and the cast-iron plants, a whole green hell with walls of waxy wet leaves, to the back deck, where we'd sit at a black metal table and eat the smoked fish with our fingers and the dip with Captain's Wafers and Crawtators, overlooking the tangled yard we were working to clear and the covered-up hot tub, which we discovered to be chock-full of leaves, lawn mower parts, and one raccoon skeleton, and which we never got working, and at the heart of it all the pale-blue heaven of the swimming pool, fiberglass walls stained with algae and peeling back in places, the bottom tiled with a snarling mosaic profile of the University of Florida gator. Whoever'd built the place had been a fan, so when you looked out at the pool you couldn't help but stare old Albert in his dinner-plate-sized eye.

When the night closed around us and the lights in the bushes switched on, Rodney would pack his bowl and light it and we would pass the pipe between us in the darkened floodlit yard. When the air was still and cool you'd hear the splash of breaching fish and, in the distance, the howls of red wolves.

The corners of my mouth would ache with salt when I smiled, and I was smiling a lot those days, especially when Rodney told stories about people I never knew, doing things

I'd never seen, in places I hadn't been to yet for the most part, or never would. Because he told those stories like I'd been there—seen and known and heard it all told and retold a million times since.

Like I belonged.

Rodney had been living in the house on Butcherpen Cove a couple months by the time I arrived. He said when the Governor reappeared, one of the first things she'd done was hand him the keys. He'd been asleep on a nasty couch in a trailer many years older than him, where he'd been staying since his last girlfriend, a DU3L widow who lived in a beach house out on 30A, called it quits. The widow had messaged him the day after he shot her husband down in a quick draw using period-accurate sixes. He'd said, I'm sorry, and she'd said, Well, I'm not. She'd been many years older than Rodney, too. Matter of fact, the only woman I ever saw stir his heart that wasn't old enough to be his mom, or at minimum a responsible babysitter, was Claudia Laval.

And we weren't talking about Claudia. Or at least I wasn't. I figured that out soon enough, after I asked him on our second full day together what'd happened with her back on the road. He didn't get mad at me or anything, didn't blow up, he just sort of gloomed over and drank for the rest of the day. That night he didn't smoke but played sad music from the speakers on the back deck and went out to the edge of the yard and shot things, some of which were really there.

I'd asked him when she was coming back and he said
never. I asked him why and that's when his face got dark. He
wouldn't answer me.

"She didn't want to get me, did she," I said.

"You?" he said. "This ain't about you." He thought about
it some more. "I mean, I don't think she was too happy about
getting in the middle of a full-fledged shootout, but she's been
in them too."

"But y'all were doing fine before you got me."

"Shit, Claudia hadn't said boo to me in about half a year."
He shook his head, stared up at the sky. "She doesn't want me
to shoot. Doesn't want me to go on DU3L anymore. I'd told
her the Gundown was my last one and, well . . ." He trailed
off, and in his voice you could tell he'd known this was a lie
before he even said it to her.

"Do you love her?"

"Course I do."

"Then why do you?"

"Love her?"

"Shoot."

Rodney thought about that for a while. "Well, in all like-
lihood it's due to my traumatic past in that I feel a need to
justify my survival by constantly putting myself at risk. But I
guess I'm also just partial to putting bullets in motherfuckers."

Not that it had done him much good. He'd barely been
able to afford the trailer he'd been crashing in, not far from

the Jenkins Inlet boat ramp. He said he hadn't showered in about two days and was just laid out in front of the window unit in his drawers, when he heard the pony car roar up. That wasn't the only thing, though. He swore before he fully woke, before he heard the engine and the tires, he'd smelled blue raspberry and burning cardboard.

He'd struggled up and gone to the door and leaned there sweating against the fiberboard with his pistol in his hand.

Movement on the other side of the door. Bootheels on the cinder-block steps and something else, something mechanical. He raised the pistol, held it.

"You won't need that," said a voice he never thought he'd hear again.

He hadn't done much work before I came, and the place was fairly run down. So were we, he said, so early in my time there we undertook improvements.

In the mornings we did push-ups and lifted rusted dumb-bells we'd found out in the shed, flexing barefoot on the spongy wood. We went to the Silver Sands Premium Outlets in Destin and returned decked out in irregular Nike and Nautica. We scooped the pool and scrubbed its walls and cleaned its traps and treated the water with chemicals bought at the pool store between the bait shop and the Waffle House until the water was a clean and perfect Powerade blue. We kept flats of such sports drinks in the kitchen, and the empties would be every-where. Fractaled plastic and black caps. The wide mouths ideal for peeing or throwing up into, if it came down to it and you were riding down the bloody highway on the way to a gunfight or something else urgent.

From June to September the gunfight action peaks, with tournaments most every week and challenges that can come at any time, so unless I went with him, I had most of the day to myself, and I didn't go with him much.

Here's what a gunfight is like: you go watch your only person in the world stand there in some old ball field with sponsor's signs flapping in the chain link, hear the gunshots of other fights and the shouts or sometimes the silences that mark their outcomes and the sounds of on-site first responders hauling off the wounded and the dead, and you stand there watching him stare down somebody who means, at best, to do him harm. That's what it's like. And then they shoot.

I did go with him to his first two challenges, though.

It was the Dakotas. They'd signed up and come on down about two weeks into my time with Rodney and when I saw them at the dueling ground—an old airstrip out by Pace—they were armed with massive red-dot scoped mule-dick pistols the likes of which I'd never seen. They wanted to fight him one by one, separate duels, but he insisted on a tandem. More points, he said to me, grinning.

But I wasn't smiling. Watching him go out to face them, I felt my life curving back towards shittiness. The knowledge that this could all end for me right now and I'd be worse than alone weighed on me something awful until Rodney drew and fired and laid the brothers out on the tarmac, screaming.

Other than that, I went with him to one tournament and as few challenges as I could help. Sometimes you couldn't avoid it and we'd be having lunch or just tooling down the road and he'd get a notification of a challenge and whip the truck around and off we'd head. Still, he figured out pretty quick that I didn't like it, though if I was gonna be laid up around the house all day on my own, he said, he wanted me to be safe.

Which meant I had to go with him to the range to practice with the Smith & Wesson M&P nine-millimeter pistol he said was mine now and I had to keep in a holster I was supposed to tote around whenever I was home. I hated that ugly-ass gun, all squared off and weirdly heavy, though I'll admit it felt better in my hand than the Glock 17 he tried on me first, and had a fair measure of styling compared to that ugly hunk of polymer in a color called Flat Dark Earth. All of Rodney's pistols were custom rebuilds he got from a gunsmith named Laramie over in Dothan, though he didn't go in for any showy outer modifications, except all his barrels were the same multicolor finish as his barrel hoods so they flashed in the sun. I made a drive out there with him once, too, heard about as much as I could stand about tread flutes and barrel lockup and magwells and shit.

I would've preferred a leaner weapon, a long-barreled revolver that made that struck-metal laser *pew* you hear in certain shows.

You want a prettier one, Rodney said when I complained, then get better at shooting.

That was some motivation, plus the fact that I wanted him to be proud. On our first range trip I fucked my grip and the gun flew back and cracked Rodney in the forehead. I looked back in horror at the blood running down between his eyes. But Rodney didn't yell, didn't rage, didn't even look upset. He just did those sad eyes at me and clenched his teeth and told me to try again. So I put in my hours till my ears hurt and my hands ached. Best I got was that my grip improved, I wasn't teacupping it anymore, but I didn't get all that much better, other than moments of sheer dumb luck, or the suspension of the laws of physics by the divine will that moves through all things, including trigger fingers and bullets.

With the Smith & Wesson accessible and Rodney off doing his thing, here I was with the whole house to myself and an in-ground pool and a tangled wild yard that backed up onto a narrow scrap of beach you could sit on and imagine yourself gigantic. I had a new phone, and Wi-Fi, and no one busting in on me, so the days piled up on each other like puppies, warm and happy. Hours in the pool, training my breath so I could dive to the bottom and touch each one of the gator's teeth. Walks alone up the blacktop road into the shopping center and back with Publix bags sagging full of snacks. Only once or twice did a carload or truckload or ragtop-Jeepload of teen-agers taunt me with a whoop. And those, I'm pretty sure, were tourists. I think most people here knew, if not who I was, then who I stayed with, and when it came to Rodney most kept a respectful distance anyway.

Except our stalker.

That's what he called her, before we knew for sure she was a she, before we knew anything much about this character who'd ride up to our property from the east, through the national seashore, except that she did so on a Honda Rancher four-wheeler modded with spotlights and a dead-rest gun mount on the front, and she was getting closer every day. Stopping in dramatic poses, scoping us out. You'd hear her 420cc single-cylinder cranking in the distance, see headlights in the trees at night, tire tracks in the sand.

She wore a red plastic batter's helmet with the name of a softball team and the logo of its sponsor business, Lips Cosmetics, a great big juicy orange kiss mark.

The first time I saw those lips clearly I said, "Dang."

"Dang is right," Rodney said.

We were out clearing vines that'd been strangling what Rodney figured were azalea bushes, spoiling the look. The stalker was down on the beach, cutting circles around an uprooted Australian pine, tires gouging up sand and shell. He squinted at her. "Guess she's a right-hander."

He meant because of the plastic earflap that went over her left cheek, but I just figured he had some special way of knowing by how she held her hands or something.

In fact she was a lefty, so I'd come to find.

"At first I thought it might be her," I said.

"Her who?" Rodney said.

"Her the Governor."

"Shit," Rodney said. "That stalker's not even out of high school." He spat into the sand, looked at me and back to the rider. "Maybe you should go talk to her."

I said maybe he should call Claudia and he said, "You first."

Turns out the vines were poison ivy and we'd been bare-handing those suckers all day. By nightfall me and him were itchy mutants, and we had to douse our sores with witch hazel for more than a week.

Meanwhile, West Florida was growing all around us. #BestFlorida bumper stickers and yard signs and those dorky cloth signs people stick in their flower beds, and red wolf decals with QR codes superglued to light poles, like one I'd seen in the grocery store parking lot, when a disappointed-looking dad tried to pick it off while his kid sat crying in the buggy with the bags.

Not long after my arrival, a special session of the Florida legislature had been called to decide Troy Yarbrough's bill. It'd taken the whole regular session just to get the thing out of committee, whatever that meant, and now you could go up to one of the red wolf decals and scan the code and it'd tell you all about their West Florida and how to make your voice heard.

We saw Troy on billboards and commercials, and in mid-May, after a particularly heated debate on the Senate floor in Tallahassee, when he was challenged by State Sen. Jonathan

Cabrera Infante to an impromptu duel, me and Rodney stood at the gas pump screen and watched the clip of him putting a bullet through the eye of the state senator from Coral Gables. "Not bad," Rodney said.

"I think the Governor could take him," I said, expecting Rodney to give me a hell-yeah grin. But he just sort of rolled his eyes and chucked the pump back into its holder, and we got back in the truck.

We were heading home from the Blackwater Bay Classic, where Rodney had taken a round to the left trap, dropping his ranking many notches. On that trip we'd passed into the zones of wholly private neighborhoods, Oleander Beach, the Villas at Anareta, upscale black sites hidden by elaborate natural and man-made blinds that were the hallmark of the movement known as New Urban Withdrawal. On the margins of these zones you wouldn't see any West Florida signage, for or against. Rodney said they wouldn't even let you cut your own grass there, they didn't care about anything, didn't believe in anything, other than everything being perfect and pretty and not having to put up with regular people and their passions. Not long after, we passed south through Garcon Point, and the road swarmed with #BestFlorida signs. I looked around, trying to study the trees. This was the land Pawpaw had bought and built on back in the nineties. This was ours, or should've been.

"Can we go look?" I asked him, meaning at the mansion and stuff.

Rodney gripped the wheel and scowled. "What good's that gonna do?"

I didn't know. Anyway, the voices I heard as the day of the vote on the bill neared were mostly raised in awe and celebration. They dared anybody to try and stop what was coming, and they were getting louder every day.

One morning Rodney woke me up flicking the light switch in my room, and said it was time for us to go see the sheriff. I asked him what the fuck did he mean, but he didn't hear me. So I dutifully pulled on my clothes and rubbed the sleep out of my eyes and stepped into my flip-flops, and we piled into Rodney's truck and drove to a ranch house on the other side of the national seashore.

Sheriff Laval was out at the paddock, raking the dirt track for rocks. Six foot three and boulder shouldered despite being in his seventies, Sheriff Laval was at the tail end of three decades of service to a county that, in his lifetime, had featured at its borders signs advising nonwhite motorists to not let the sun set on their black asses here. He was also Claudia's dad.

"Sheriff," Rodney said as we approached the paddock, and the big man dusted himself off and stood there with his hands on his waist, taking us both in. Me in my shorts and flips and Rodney with bandages peeking out from the neck of his shirt.

"This must be the boy," Sheriff Laval said, and he reached across the fence and shook my hand, which has never felt smaller or squishier, though the sheriff wasn't the type who needed to crush your hand to show how bad he was. Nor have I ever been prouder than when the big man looked from me to Rodney and back and said, "Hell, I'm seeing double."

He'd said it with a smile, but as though the joke was floating on top of something deep and sad as hell. I didn't care. The sadness was between the two of them, and they had plenty to go around.

Once we were seated at his kitchen table with mugs of black coffee in front of us, Sheriff Laval cut to the chase. "You talked to Claudia lately?" he said.

"Not for a couple weeks."

"Me neither."

"What's she mad at you about?"

Sheriff Laval said, outside of the general daddy-daughter situation, which is fraught and liable to blow up at any time, Claudia was pissed at him because he'd come out in support of Yarbrough's bill. Rodney sighed but must've known better than to make a case about it, and he kept his mouth shut until Sheriff Laval said, "What about you? Still doing that gunfighting?"

"Yes, sir."

"You intend to keep on with it?"

"Got the Jackson County Invitational next week."

"Sounds like how the cockfights used to be. Dogfights. All that shit had names like that. 'The Lee County Derby.'" Sheriff Laval trailed off, into the bloodsports of the seventies and eighties.

"I won about two thousand dollars at the last one."

"Two thousand dollars and you took how much lead?" His eyes roved up and down Rodney's body. All the places he knew his almost-son had been shot.

"It's not something you make a living at," the sheriff went on. "It's something you pay for. And you're gonna keep on paying."

You could look at the man's face and see he wasn't being mean. It hurt him. Gnawed at him. I think, like most grown people do about the kids they raised, he believed it was all his fault.

Rodney had moved in with Claudia and her folks shortly after the massacre, and back then, he was a real disaster. Then– Lance Corporal Laval and his wife had known Grandma Krista since back in high school, and they had stayed friends despite Krista being inexorably drawn to breaking rules. When Rodney lived with them, the rules were doors open at all times, which meant Claudia didn't have to squeak a hinge to slip in there and spoon Rodney till he stilled.

Didn't always work, though, and he'd be up and so freaked, still living in that long and bloody night, that it'd draw the grown Lavals upstairs and they'd do what they could to contain him. Daytime, you'd have to watch if you were unloading the dishes and taking a knife to the block and he was anywhere nearby.

One weekend morning, when none of them had slept much, Rodney had looked up hollow eyed from his cereal bowl and asked Sheriff Laval if he could teach him.

"Teach what?"

"Teach me how to shoot."

Sheriff Laval studied him for a moment. This white boy in his house. He'd taught Rodney how to shoot, or at least how to handle a gun, back when he was little. He'd taken him to the range or out back to ping beer cans off the fence posts. But this was different, and the big man knew it.

"Son, are you trying to go kill a whole bunch of people?"

Rodney's eyes and voice cut low.

"No, sir," he said. "I just don't want it to happen again."

The sheriff had finished chewing and pressed his hands to the tabletop and pushed himself up. "All right, then," he said to Rodney. "Let's go to work."

Out in the yard, in the woods, on the sands, he'd train Rodney until his hand ached from recoil. Train him on the pull and the sight. How to cover a room.

"Now fetch that brass," Sheriff Laval would say, and Rodney would gather up the casings with throbbing fingers, spend hours priming and reloading them.

Rodney never got famous, not for gunfighting. Never fought one of the greats. He saw a few notable engagements, though, and was caught in a shootout once between Golden Eli's entourage and this whole family who'd come to watch, thinking their dumbass cousin could put down the best in the business. When the gunfire stopped and the bodies littered the parking lot, Golden Eli, with the pistol still in his hand, had brushed back the flat brim of his glittering ballcap from where it'd fallen over his eye, turned across the parking lot to Rodney, crouched beside his truck a couple rows over, and given him that legendary smile.

That's how we are in this family. We brush up with greatness, or maybe greatness glances off of us and keeps on streaking toward forever, leaving us behind, all weird and unfulfilled. Maybe gunfighting was Rodney's way of trying to catch it, or maybe it was just his way of passing time on the way to the grave.

The first person he'd challenged was this paunchy middle-aged machinist out in Pace who Rodney figured he could take, and earned himself a baby-fist-sized patch of scar tissue on his left hip for his arrogance, to match the five puckered lips of old stab wounds on his back. Yet he survived and the machinist from Pace was dead before he hit the pavement, so one of the on-site EMTs assured him afterwards, Rodney's first shot having lipped the lower right shoulder of the guy's chest armor and torn straight through to his heart. The second shot, taken as the guy fell, caught his throat and sent a fount of blood so far and arcing that, even though they were both shit-tier competitors and the contest would have no bearing on the divisional, much less the state rankings, the clip became one of DU3L's most viewed that entire season. In DU3L at the time, the state of Florida had only two divisions: Southern and Central, with a statewide final ranking compiled at season's end, which burned up the panhandle competitors like Rodney, who were forced to compete in Central. While he wasn't exactly on the map, this performance set the table for his next four gunfights and his climb into the Central division's top sixteen.

The top sixteen overall in pistols, that is. Top five in paced duels and top ten in quick draw. Rodney didn't fuck with longarms, and there was no way he was meeting anyone with swords—he said the fights took forever and never looked as cool as the guys who swung them hoped. That summer, DU3L would introduce a fixed-blade knife league, but that shit looked more like wrestling, all close and intimate and groping, and anyway he'd been stabbed enough before.

He fought his next four challenges in abandoned airstrips and between the light poles of parking lots and in the atrium of the old Cordova Mall in Pensacola, where as a small child he'd walked hand in hand with the people who loved him in the glory of the early 2000s, all of whom had died or disappeared in what the news had called a massacre but to Rodney was the beginning of hell.

By summer he'd challenged his first five opponents, and the weeks to come would see him take on his first five challengers. That's the rule. You have to challenge five out the gate, and then you get to wait around while random gunmen challenge you. The two-week waiting period between challengers was intended to avoid mismatches between grief-blind relatives and seasoned killers, but that didn't always work out. It's like dating, he told me later. You get a match and you can look at their picture, scope out their details all you want, but you don't know until you're squared up with them in the real world.

So he'd fought and fought, and he'd won. Found himself at peace in a way he hadn't felt since before the massacre.

Problem was, he'd made a promise. Back when the sheriff had taught him how to shoot, he'd promised the big man that he'd give the law a chance when he got older. Which he'd tried, dropping in and out of cop training throughout his twenties, and now he was promising someone else—Claudia.

He never told me exactly how it happened with her. I can't imagine trying to sneak around in Sheriff Laval's house, even if you're horned-up teenagers and out of your minds with love, but suffice to say the two of them got together and what formed between them stuck. He was never over her, and she put up with him through his dropouts and fuckups and meltdowns as a grown-ass man, until he came upon DU3L.

Rodney wasn't an early adopter—there weren't many of them left—but he'd watched with growing interest as the app DU3L launched and garnered interest and participants, watched the duelists' streams and those of commentators, watched as sanctioned dueling grounds sprang up across the litter-strewn untenanted properties of Opportunity Zones across the panhandle and the alleys behind disused strip malls sang with gunfire. He took his own weapons to the range with greater frequency and copied the stances he'd seen, until he finally said fuck it, signed the papers, paid the fees, submitted his pistols to DU3L for inspection and chipping. After a trial period and the acceptance of a likeness rights agreement and insurance policies, he officially joined.

When he told Claudia he'd done it, when it was too late, she'd said, No, nope, done. This was a bridge too far and her ass wasn't crossing it with him. He'd tried to fight with her about it, ask her what was the difference between this and what she did, when in the course of a routine traffic stop some nasty motherfucker could whip out a pistol and shoot her dead, or when she could just be blasted off the side of the road by a careless driver, and for what?

When Rodney told me about this, I asked him, Well, what'd she say?

He laughed, said she told him what he could go and do and he had another thing coming if he thought she was going to wait around for him to die.

That's what love's about, though, right? he'd said.

His voice had cracked in the telling and the truth is, we're never really done with love. Or love's never done with us. Before they'd shown up on Big Mike's doorstep, Claudia hadn't spoken to Rodney for almost six months. He'd been living out of a trailer in Navarre and she'd been promoted to corporal. She was a couple of hours into a weeklong vacation that should've seen her board a plane for Cabo with two of her girlfriends when he ran into her one night at Jenny Haverford's Bermuda Deep Bar & Grill and they'd stayed there all night talking, like they used to when they were kids. By dawn he'd convinced her to come to New Orleans with him for the Gundown.

On the way home from Sheriff Laval's, Rodney pulled us off for gas. I had to do the pumping because he was still pretty sore. He'd insisted he be the one to drive, though, and he got out and leaned hissing against the hood of the truck while I pumped the gas.

While the tank filled, a breeze picked up from the north, and I felt the grit before I saw the color of the air change, first a blush pink and then something closer to a burnt orange and, with the wind mounting, the air around us went red. The grit in the wind stung my eyes and I could see Rodney wincing even behind his sunglasses as we felt the grains of what I'd later learn to be red clay gathering around us. There was a drought up in Georgia, evidently—had been for years, but now it was getting bad, they said—the red clay soil, sapped of moisture, went dusty and lifted in the winds that blew down on them sometimes. It was worse up near the border, where there was no gulf to kick up its own bands of wind and drive the red clouds off. Worse still in Alabama, but what wasn't?

"Look," I said, pointing with my free hand to the bollard up in front of the pump. Slapped across it was a sticker that said GO WEST. Not #BESTFLORIDA or ONE FLORIDA or any of that shit.

"It's one of ours," I said.

"So what," Rodney said.

"So," I said, "you think she's back?"

He spat ocher and shook his head as I squeezed the last few gallons into the tank. "Maybe she is. Or maybe she'll be gone another ten years. Maybe she'll stay gone."

They'd grown up together at the house in Tiger Cove, but there were big chunks of time when her mom would fall in love with some dude and they'd move, move in with him. A couple weeks or months later, sure enough, they'd be back, sometimes in trouble, hiding out like the house was Fort Apache, and, according to Rodney, there'd be these wonderful days of preparation, of imagined siege. Or else they'd have some loser guy in tow, which my grandma didn't always care for but put up with anyway because if there was one thing Grandma Krista dearly loved, more than West Florida, more than the sun and the sand, it was Alexis, her same-age stepdaughter, and these kids they'd raised together.

When Rodney was in middle school and Destiny was a junior, she would go to his school whenever there was a bomb threat or a shooter drill and find him outside where all the kids had been herded. She'd come across the sports fields and lead him off to wander through burning swales of blacktop, behind the Sam's Club to the west of the middle school campus, to squat amid the loading bays and dumpsters filled with loss, Destiny passing him half-smoked Marlboro Lights while she told him what she was in trouble for now.

She'd be there causing havoc one day and then gone the next, so when Rodney had woken up in the hospital the day after the massacre and they told him what had happened to his family and that Destiny was gone, he wasn't exactly shocked. Not about that or the fact that it looked like she had torn through their attackers like a living engine of destruction. He said to a nurse that before he passed out while being stabbed, he'd seen a razor-sharp light enclose him.

For a long, long time, through his convalescence, he believed she'd come back any day now. I asked him where he thought she went, for all those years, and he told me she was off doing some Gandalf shit.

"You didn't ask her?"

"Of course I did," Rodney said.

"Well, what'd she tell you?"

"Some crazy shit," he said. "You know how she is."

Rodney told me once that when the Governor was small, one of her mom's boyfriends believed she was a kind of demon. The beast of the end of the world, he said. Those were the man's actual words. He'd be hanging around the house in Tiger Cove and find her in the living room pretending to watch cartoons or whatever, and it'd be like a leopard was sitting there, or some old-time derangement of an angel. Alexis soon dumped him for unrelated reasons, but even when his life was freed from her presence, the believer had taken it upon himself to perform reconnaissance on this possible Antichrist, and he began to shadow her movements daily, appearing at the bus stop where she waited in the mornings by herself on a wedge of grass, parking his car in stakeout across the street from the playground of her school. He didn't know exactly what he was looking for, but he made notes of the strange things he saw, or the ordinary things that, in her proximity, took on new and terrible significance. Children dropping unprovoked from the monkey bars; a lightning strike on the softball field not twenty feet away from him, a colossal explosion and everything gone stunning white, then rain and smoke and the vision of the girl across the street, standing just outside the group of children who'd been herded there. Reports of her ex's behavior reached Alexis and he was banned from the vicinity of the school, threatened with the law. But then it was hurricane season, 2004, and Hurricane Ivan came barreling down upon West Florida, and the believer, on his recon rounds on the eve of the storm, could've sworn he heard Destiny's name on the mounting wind and whispers of the great day of her wrath, so on the eve of landfall, he'd gone to the door of the house in Tiger Cove and tried to warn Alexis and Krista, done what he thought was a favor.

What he got in return was the Colt jammed in his face and a warning not to show his ass around here or anywhere near this girl again, or else. He slunk off that time, but they didn't leave it to chance. They said you couldn't, when it came to fucked-up men. When the storm was through and half the region lay in ruins, including their house, Alexis and Krista drove through the wreckage-strewn streets and came at him alone and unsuspecting one powerless night.

The motherfucking Puma Sisters, Rodney called them, smiling.

You could find them poolside or on the beach any given day. Alexis's skin perpetually burned. She didn't want to glow or gleam. She wanted to be like something taken out of a smelter, translucent with heat. If you were going to look at her, she wanted it to hurt.

Grandma Krista's tan, on the other hand, was award winning and might as well have been bone deep, layered evenly like lacquer. What the ads at the time called the Savage Tan. To see them both together you might've thought the sun above was nothing but a hole eaten out of the sky by their own ravenous light.

I guess I get my skin from Grandma Krista because after a couple weeks in the heart of West Florida I was burnished brown and my eyes were shocking white.

Crazy eyes, Rodney would joke, like he was one to talk.

On Memorial Day, Rodney was off at the Jackson County Applewhite Tactical Invitational, so I was flying solo at the house. For the past few weeks I'd been even more on my own than usual. I'd wake up around noon and hit the pool and lay out for most of the day until Rodney came back home, if he did at all. He would be gone now for days at a time, and you could tell a change had come upon him. Lately, Rodney had been seeming anxious, like how he'd get before a gunfight, but different, because before a gunfight he'd never get these bursts of elation, start bopping around the house, dancing with himself, doing a fair amount more grooming than usual.

I'd been swimming all morning, getting chased by water spiders jumping my wake on leaves, not really thinking about the fact that a swarm of birds were diving and cackling at our little beach. I'd been cadging nugs from Rodney's jar and sipping Gulfs until they got too warm and I'd go and crack a fresh one, just laying out by the pool all day. By noon I was lost to myself. I thought there might be fireworks, so I slipped on my flips and a shirt Rodney had gotten at the Blackwater River Invitational and went down to our little beach, where I pulled up the bottom of a flotsam Rubbermaid cooler and sat atop it watching the bay and beyond.

Then I realized it was still daytime and sat there feeling pretty stupid for a while but also pretty good, when I heard the familiar sound of the stalker's engine through the trees down the beach.

She was heading my way at a good clip, weaving through the cypress knees, skirting the surf, water sparkling in her wake. Now I saw she wasn't going to stop, and she didn't until she was about ten yards away from me and I could smell the gasoline and see the water beaded on her bare forearms.

She had work gloves on, the ends rolled down around her wrists, faded jeans and a yellow T-shirt that said De Luna Fest 2016, the screen print cracking like dried mud. Her nose was flat and her eyes were furious, framed in the piecey ends of a dark-brown haircut that poofed out of her batting helmet.

I stood up and Rodney's T-shirt was so big the hem hit me midthigh, covering my trunks, so I must've looked half-naked, or like I was going for the boyfriend fit, because the stalker sort of looked away, just for a second, then she snapped right back, leaned across the handlebars of her Rancher, fingers brushing the rifle in a dead-rest rack mounted to the front.

"Tell me the truth," she said. "You killed it or that guy you live with killed it."

"Killed what?" I said, suddenly sorry I wasn't wearing the holster like Rodney said I should.

She glared at me with blast-furnace eyes.

"You don't know?" she said.

The engine was ticking down, thick metallic clicks that made me think of how Rodney would work the cylinder of a revolver.

I shook my head and she said, Well, there was a dolphin up the beach a ways with a bullet in its head. Hadn't I seen the birds?

Sure enough, over her shoulder there was a flock of gulls diving down the beach.

I said I'd never killed anything, much less a dolphin, and in fact had seen a family of them when I first moved here and it was so beautiful it made me cry, which was true. I'd been out at the Surf & Sun with Rodney, sipping Bushwhackers, when I saw the fins break the water. Thought I'd never catch my breath.

She sized me up for so long that I thought she might ask me to tell my story right then and there, but instead she just said, Well, you wanna go see it? meaning the dead dolphin, and I said sure, and before I knew it I was riding on the back of her Rancher, hovering my arm around her waist as she drove, a big fan of surf kicking up on our left.

Her name was Leona Odom and she lived with her grandma on the other side of the national seashore, about a mile's ride up the beach and through some swampy woods. They had a paddock and corral and an honest-to-god barn where they boarded horses for people. She'd had horses, too, but both of them had died of strangles the year before. Her great-grandma had come from Okinawa with her Marine grandpa in the forties and raised a family that got picked off in much the same way as mine. Grandma had been a member of the campus revolutionaries, over at the University of West Florida, in Pensacola. Worked on the staff of the underground magazine *Fish Cheer*. She and others who had posters in their rooms of VC women with AK-47s had occupied the library and from its roof unfurled a banner that read FUCK ROTC.

The dead dolphin was lying on its side, wedged by the tide against some cypress knees, mouth open, nubby teeth showing.

"Shit," I said, looking from the dolphin to her. "What the fuck."

"Like I said, somebody shot it in the head."

"Who shoots a dolphin?"

"If it wasn't y'all," she said, teasing her theory out, "then I think it's those West Florida fuckers. This isn't the first dead dolphin like this I found."

I stood there blinking like, Hold up.

"What West Florida fuckers?" I asked. "There's more than one kind."

Leona cocked her head to the side and scanned me, said, "Go on."

I told her the short version of who my family was and everything, how I'd ended up here. Told her about the Governor.

She thought it over a while.

"You sure it's a robot arm?" she said.

"I'm not sure it's just the arm," I said.

"And y'all don't want West Florida to be, like, Jesus paradise?"

I said not that I knew of and she asked if we were cool with this and that and where the Woolsack version of West Florida stood on trans kids and I said from what I understood West Florida meant you could be whoever you were in your heart—but I could ask to be sure.

"Well," she said, "I'm talking about the Troy Yarbrough kind." She pointed across the bay towards Garcon Point. "I see his yacht or whatever out here sometimes," she went on. "It's like a big black speedboat."

"That's his?" I said. I'd seen the low sharp black thing racing over the waves. It looked mean and expensive as hell, but I'd never seen a soul on it except once, a woman in a red crochet cover-up holding on to the rail.

"Fuck that guy," I said.

"Right? Dolphins are super intelligent. It's so gross."

I agreed they were. "You'd think they'd stop swimming up to the boat, though. If they keep getting shot whenever they do."

"Freaking people are intelligent, too, allegedly, and we keep getting ourselves shot."

I thought about Rodney and where he was at that moment and I got real quiet.

"So," Leona said after a while, trying to change the subject and settling on her ride, which she clapped with one hand proudly as she asked me, "do you like four-wheelers?"

I said no but that I thought hers was pretty cool.

"You shoot?" she said.

"Not really."

She squinted at me. Thumbed up the brim of her batting helmet. Shook her head. "I guess you don't have to with him around."

"Who, Rodney?"

"The crazy guy. The shooter."

"He's not a shooter," I said. "He's a gunfighter."

"Well, yeehaw, motherfucker," and she spun invisible pistols on her hip. I was quiet for a while and she added, "Is he your dad or something?"

"Something like that."

He wasn't crazy, I wanted to say but didn't. Sure, I heard him scream awake more mornings than I'd like, and the other day he'd lurched home at ten a.m. with this mark on his forehead like it was Ash Wednesday, only the ashes were red and in, like, a claw slash. I asked him what was that shit on his head and he lurched past me, hands hanging heavy at his sides, like a cracker golem, heading for his room. He said over his shoulder that he'd see me in the morning and I said it *was* morning, but he didn't answer.

"If you'd been through what he went through," I explained to Leona O., "you'd seem crazy, too."

"Which is what?" she said.

So I told her.

"Well, fucking jeez," Leona said. "Now I feel like a jerk."

"Don't," I said. "It's not your fault."

She chewed on that for a while until the flies got loud, buzzing around the dolphin's blowhole like a nasty little tornado.

"What should we do with it?" I said finally.

She said, "We're gonna give it a proper burial."

Which we did, on the beach, in a hole that took till sundown to dig with shovels from her shed, me and Leona standing in a waist-deep hole, chucking sand into a big pile we'd have to shovel back in once we'd rolled the dolphin in and she'd said some words.

I stood beside her while she spoke, my bare legs sand flecked, my hands locked in front of me like they're supposed to be at a funeral.

"Do you like horses?" she said finally.

"Big time," I lied.

"I wish I still had horses," she said. "But now it's just me and Bonaparte."

"Bonaparte."

She chucked her shovel aside and went over to her four-wheeler and gave its flank a clap. She'd named the vehicle that because he was small yet fierce and because she'd had a pony called that once upon a time.

When we'd finished the service she rode me back to my beach. By then the stars were out and the drone show was about to start. You could see them rising from the opposite shore, hundreds, lit and gyring. I went and got us drinks from the house, and I sat on the Rubbermaid and she sat on Bonaparte's saddle and we watched the drones flock and swarm, making patriotic shapes and messages in the sky over the bay.

A great big kitchen knife of moonlight laid out over the water, pointing towards me. My toes were in the wet sand and there was nothing in front of us but the water and in the distance, through the dark, the bluffs and under them, to the west, Bayou Texar, East Hill, Pensacola and to the east, Garcon Point. Troy Yarbrough's camp. The false West Florida.

In a matter of months the land across the bay would look like burners in a gas grill switched on high. For now there were just dock lights and house lights and one or two boats and planes sparkling the dark up.

Leona told me how her mom was dead and her dad was gone but hadn't killed her. Her dad had been all fucked up on the same shit that'd killed my Aunt Amber, and Leona's mom had fallen out of love with him and in love with someone else, this horse masseur who visited their barn sometimes and laid hands and crystals on the beasts. Leona's mom had the horses and the makeup-and-nail store, Lips, from the softball helmet, and when her fucked-up husband threatened her with divorce she'd cleaned out her bank accounts and hidden about thirty thousand dollars with a friend over in Navarre. Another horse lady, Leona's godmother. This lady was some kind of half-ass barrel racer and stood four foot eight inches tall in ropers. Turns out her godmom coveted those thousands and bore a great simmering resentment for cheaters too, and so one day she lured Leona's mom out to her property with the promise of a trail ride and shot her and buried her and kept the money herself.

"Jesus," I said. "I'm sorry."

"You don't have to be," she said. "That half-pint cup of bitch is dead."

I didn't know what to say, so I said I had to pee.

"Did you ever get the money?" I asked as we walked through the yard to the house.

"Some things are worth more than money."

I agreed with that and let her in the sliding glass door, which I left open behind us in case it seemed creepy to close it. I didn't care about the bugs that'd come swarming in to the cool and the light. I waited in the living room, doing the little-kid pee dance while she went to the hall bathroom, and when she came back I took my turn.

When I came out I thought maybe she wouldn't be there, that this was the part that would finally reveal it all to be a dream and I'd wake back up in what was finally, irrevocably Louisiana, in the life I'd known before, but when I stepped out of the hall bathroom to the sustained roar of the toilet tank, which did that all the time, I saw not only was she still there but she was sitting on the couch with her arms folded, legs crossed. I could see the fine hairs on her forearms, bleached white by the sun.

"Did you jiggle it?" Leona said.

"What?"

"I asked did you jiggle it."

I took a half step back, said, "I didn't . . . I don't . . ."

She laughed. Uncrossed her legs and arms and leaned forward. "I meant the handle of the commode, dumbass. Go and jiggle it and that'll stop the water running."

"Oh," I said.

But I didn't move.

I just stood there listening to the sound of water rushing in the tank.

"Go on," she said. "Or do you need me to help?"

Well, I did, and afterwards we watched the sky where the fireworks should have been but weren't. When I went back inside for more drinks I brought a present for her. One of the Governor's cards.

"Awesome," Leona said, turning the card over in her hands. "I always wanted to be from somewhere that isn't real."

Then she smiled at me so that I'd know she didn't really mean that. The fireworks weren't real either, but we pretended to watch them, pointed at them, followed their trails of smoke and light over the bay. Like the MOAB Rodney had told me about not long before. How when he was six years old Alexis took him and Kenan and Destiny to see the detonation of the most powerful nonnuclear bomb ever on U.S. soil. The GBU-43/B Massive Ordnance Air Blast, or as it would be popularly known, the MOAB—the Mother of All Bombs. Eighteen thousand pounds of TNT, more than Hiroshima, a place he had no clue about but whose name made his half sister's voice crackle with dread. She'd picked him up from school, like she did in those days when his mom was at work, and said she had it in her mind to see the bomb. She'd been warned about its destructive reach. Whether power would be affected in the surrounding towns was a question. Whether windows or teeth would be shaken loose and boats would roll atop the sea. She thought the best place to witness the blast would be the picnic area at the foot of the Garcon Point Bridge, and only when they'd been there for a while balanced on riprap boulders did they learn that the detonation had occurred hours earlier. The great thing had happened and nobody had felt a thing.

But because of the way brains work, Rodney had a clear memory of seeing the bomb, the flash of light on a distant shore, and the mushroom cloud rising after it.

Later, he would sit in an angry knot on the floor of his room playing a game where, if he got the assault or specialist strike package and managed a twenty-five-person kill streak unassisted, he would be awarded with the Mother of All Bombs. Two years after the massacre, the bomb would be utilized in combat, dropped on a system of tunnels in northwest Afghanistan.

I didn't tell Rodney about Leona O. until a couple days later. He came back from the invitational unwounded and took me out to the Surf & Sun, the old motor court out on Pensacola Beach, the following day for fried grouper bites and Bushwhackers, like it was old times. Only you could tell something was haunting him, drawing him back.

We were sitting outside at a bright-pink high-top table, overlooking the volleyball setup and the thatched cabana where a woman in an old Big Johnson shirt was mixing drinks, when Rodney's phone pinged with a challenge. His fifth.

The guy was fifteen minutes down the road. Rodney didn't even hesitate before replying.

While Rodney leaned at the high-top, stewing, waiting for the guy to show, I told him about Leona in one burst. Only, instead of being proud like I thought he'd be, Rodney got in my face. Tried to warn me.

"Don't let yourself get fucked up with that love shit," he said.

I just watched the thatched cabana wherefrom our drinks appeared in little cups.

The waitress looked at me, held up the drink, said, "You old enough for this?"

Rodney snorted. "Guess he's old enough for everything now."

The waitress set our drinks down, and when she left he resumed getting on me.

"Don't bring her ass up in the house when I'm not around."

I said, "OK," robot-style.

Rodney said, "I don't need to catch a freaking charge. Underage kids in my house doing god knows what."

"I'm sorry," I said, but he didn't seem to hear me.

"Number two," he said, "don't let that little bitch get you all fucked up thinking you're the one and only. News flash, motherfucker: you aren't. I don't care if she shows up with a pregnancy test with a line on it. You go buy four and you make her piss on all of them."

I looked at him, this stranger, and said, "What the fuck?"

"That's what they fucking do, man, and you need to understand that shit."

"Do what?"

"They fucking lie. Like your fuckin' mom did."

"Lie about what?" I said.

"Nothing," he said, looking away.

"No," I said, voice getting louder. "Lie about what?"

Rodney's phone pinged again. The challenger was here. He stood up, finished his drink. "You're gonna find out your own damn way anyhow," he said, then he walked off to the car to get his gun rig on.

The gunfight occurred in the ruins of a former motor court just up the road, out behind a jag of crumbling pink cinder block. The guy was just some asshole in a jersey bedecked with scowling long-toothed skulls and black pants of many pockets. A camo ball cap with a frayed bill shadowing an old pair of wraparound Oakleys, whose frames were dusted with the green particulate remnants of mowed lawns. The guy was apparently local, originally from out on Blackwater Bay, but had moved away for years and only just returned, like many who'd begun to flock back to the panhandle counties in the summer and fall of that year.

I stood off in the surf and watched with my arms folded, not because I was mad but because I didn't want this guy, or especially Rodney, to see I was shaking.

The guy stood with his back to a concrete extension that'd once housed an air-conditioning unit. There was nothing behind Rodney but a few low humps of cinder block peeking out of the sand, tangles of rebar and parking barriers, nothing that would take a stray shot or keep one from doing damage up the beach, which he saw now, when he glanced back for a moment, was scattered with people in the distance.

"How about we move," Rodney said.

"The fuck for?"

Rodney jerked his head back to indicate the people in the distance. "So you don't hit somebody when you miss."

The guy plucked at his shirt collar where it peeked over the neckline of his armor, which was cheap plate and fixed with a holster in the center of his chest, which Rodney always said was the sign of a bullshitter. "Bitch," the guy said, "you're the one's gonna miss."

But Rodney was already walking down toward the water, through the sand churned with vape cartridges and knotted plastic bags of dog shit, to stand with his back to the gulf where the sun had sunk for the moment into a cloud bank, waves of purpling red above a sea of gold. The man walked reluctantly over to a place in the cinder-block wall that faced him, and as he did, I eased over, out of the line of fire, and glimpsed the scabby raised scars at the corners of the man's sunglasses.

Karenia scars, I figured, as the man took up his stance, still talking shit. It bummed me out somewhat to think that this guy had suffered in the past, and was maybe even a dumb and reckless motherfucker as a result of his past suffering. But if you started thinking that way, Rodney said, then there was nobody you could bring yourself to shoot.

"I'm gonna set the count, all right?" Rodney reached for his phone.

The man grunted, jouncing from one leg to the other. Rodney eased into his own stance, the wind from offshore cool at his back. In the distance, the sun was still falling through the clouds.

He eyed the man and felt the flecks of sea spray, windborne.

The cell membranes of *Karenia letalis*, the microscopic organism responsible for deaths years back on Blackwater Bay and elsewhere since, are fragile things, and when broken by cresting waves they fracture into particles, lighter than air, smaller than light, invisible, floating with the sea spray onshore.

On Rodney's chest the phone began its countdown ping. The other man drew his pistol, a chromed Desert Eagle, just a monstrous mule dick of a weapon. Rodney wanted to ask him where he'd stolen it, but he just listened to the waves and the pings counting down to . . . five . . . four . . . three . . .

The shadows on the beach fled and his own stretched out before him, cast by the sun which had now fallen from the clouds and shone blazing over his shoulders. Twin orbs of fire in the lenses of the Oakleys.

. . . two . . . one . . .

They stood still as framed photographs there on the beach, as the last ping sounded and the sun spat a wave of radiation at them. Before the ping had ceased, the man jabbed his Eagle's muzzle forward, as if to force away the glare, and fired. The shot kicked up surf to Rodney's left, but he didn't see it—he squeezed his own shots off and the man fell in a tangle of limbs, thrashing, screaming in the sand.

The first week of June, Sheriff Laval invited us over for coffee again. The yard and the house looked no different, but the second we came in you knew something had changed. The sheriff had something he needed to say, we could see it straining to get out. He squared his shoulders and propped his elbows on the countertop across from Rodney and said, "I got an invitation for you."

"To what?"

"There's gonna be a party," he said. "Out at Garcon Point. To celebrate the passing of the bill."

Rodney looked at him. "It hasn't passed yet."

"Just a matter of time," the sheriff said. The vote was coming that Friday and they'd run the numbers every way they could, and any way you sliced it Troy Yarbrough's bill was going to the governor's desk in Tallahassee. After that it'd go to D.C., to Congress, and then it was anybody's game, but right here and now they were sitting on the verge of victory. "I think it's time you got in good with these people, with Troy. He really wants to meet you."

Rodney's mouth went tight. "What's he want? Permission to take my family's whole idea?"

"He wants you to be a part of it."

Rodney got an odd, dreamy look. "Who says I'm not?"

"Nobody's saying anything except it's time you quit this shooting business."

"What about Claudia?"

"What about her?"

"I guess she hasn't changed her mind."

"Not about you, and not about me, and not about West Florida."

"Guess we're in the same boat, then."

"Guess so," said the sheriff. He sipped his coffee. "So, you coming?"

Rodney looked at me and I was trying to tell him NO with my eyes but he told Sheriff Laval he'd think about it, and he sure did because by nightfall he was so fucked up he was calling out for me on the deck. I'd been up in my room texting with Leona. I was planning on walking down to her place later, but then I'd told her about how me and Rodney were probably going to a party at Troy Yarbrough's and she was mad and even though I mostly didn't want to go, I'd ended up arguing for why we should, like it'd been my idea. And so I was mad too, and worse, here was Rodney hollering for me to come out there.

When I did, he was down in the yard with his gun rig strapped around his waist, boxers hanging off his chicken legs, swaying.

"Get me two cans," he said.

"The bird?"

"The tin kind, Rally, goddamn."

I looked around for some beer cans. Depending on how bad things had gotten that particular day, I wouldn't have to go far. We usually kept the place clean because respecting the land is an essential part of loving your state, but lately, the worse Rodney got, the less I think he believed the state was beautiful and worthy of love, and there were beer cans scattered around the pool and up under the lip of the deck in the pine straw, where the weights sat rusting. Meanwhile, my phone was in my bed getting blown up by Leona.

"OK," Rodney said, when I had a pair of cans, Gulf Lites, sun-bleached silver. "Now toss them in the yard."

I just stood there, holding the cans.

Rodney had the heels of his hands on the grips of the pistols hanging at his hips. "Toss those cans in the yard, man. I'm gonna walk these bastards all the way across the street."

So I tossed and he drew and fired, and sure enough those bastards rolled and rolled.

I stood back, in the roar and after-roar, waiting for the cops, who didn't come.

But Leona did. Rolled up the next day around noon on Bonaparte to see, she said, if I was still alive. She rode furious right up the path from our beach and through the pine trees and the yard, tearing up the sod I'd laid, all the way to the edge of the pool, where I was hanging with my elbows propped. She cut the throttle and climbed out of the saddle and flicked the strap at her chin and yanked her helmet off and hung it on the handlebar and stood there with her hands on her hips, glaring at me.

"Hey," I said.

"So," she said, "you're alive."

She was pissed. Anyone could see that. But Leona looked mad, and in a different way than the time with the dolphin.

When people say they want to know you're still alive, that usually means they're so pissed off at you that once they confirm you're alive, they might just kill your ass themselves.

"I'm sorry," I said. "I don't really want to go. But it's family, you know?"

"They're fuckers," Leona said, stepping out of her Keds. I figured she meant Troy Yarbrough and company, but who knows. She walked over to where I was leaning at the edge of the pool, and she sat down and dangled her legs in the water.

"Is he coming back soon?"

"Nah," I said, and slipped beneath the surface, drifting down to the bottom of the pool with the leaves and the bugs and the frog bones. Then I kicked my way up and did a mermaid breach, tossed my hair back and swam over to Leona, who regarded me with still-mad eyes but a little flicker of approval in the corners of her mouth.

"When's he coming home?"

I said I didn't know, but not soon. The duel at the Surf & Sun had marked Rodney's last challenge, and the next tournament wasn't until Fourth of July weekend, but once he'd sobered up in the morning, he'd said he had to go out anyway, put his range hours in. Only he hadn't brought any of his gear other than the pistol he wore, and when I texted him at noon he said he was gonna be gone late, not to wait up.

"I don't know where the hell he's been going," I said, but hey, we had the house to ourselves and would until way later.

She said that was cool and for the rest of the afternoon, we smoked and swam, and then we went inside. I slid the door shut and put the broomstick in that locked it and I turned the blinds shut and we laid out on the couch in the cool dark, pulsing with residual heat. We smoked and laid there watching nothing, reading our phones, and I was starting to feel a double edge of danger to the situation because, while Rodney probably wouldn't be coming home, there was a chance he would. And the thought of it filled me with both fear and a kind of bursting joy, the idea that if he just met Leona he'd see how great she was. I wondered how he could live with me, even with as little time as he'd been spending around the place, and not see the glow she put on me, how she made me feel.

Then it hit me and I understood.

"He's in love," I said.

"Who?"

"Rodney. That's where he's been. That's why he's been acting all weird, weirder."

Leona got a look on her face I'd never seen before. Like she was holding me with her eyes over a bottomless pit and whether she let me go depended on what I'd say. "You're more than just his weird bastard child, you know," she said.

"Then what else am I?" I said.

She couldn't tell me, so I went to get us a couple Powerades. When I came back she was sitting up with the TV on, the remote in her hand.

"Look," she said and pointed to the television.

There on the sixty-inch screen was the cover art for *Scorpion Beach* (1997), and there was Grandma Krista front and center in a black slingshot swimsuit and a cross between a life jacket and a bulletproof vest, standing in the saddle of a Sea-Doo 9700 modded with fiberglass plates for a mecha effect, staring out with reckless eyes and her teeth bared, ready to rip. In the movie she was second-in-command to Julie Strain's leader of a postapocalyptic girl gang caught up in a convoluted time travel plot involving a rival gang of delinquent girls, a detective with a troubled past, a space-time cult, and sacrificial murder in New Miami.

"For real?" I said.

"Come on," Leona said. "You know you want to."

And I did. Ever since I'd moved here, I'd tried to get Rodney to watch some of Grandma Krista's stuff with me, like so he could point out if this or that tic was inherited or maybe just tell me some stories about his mom, but he never wanted to. At first he wouldn't say why, but when I pressed him long enough he finally admitted it was because he didn't want to see her die. She died in most of those movies. Blasted by mutant gangsters. Eaten by stock-footage sharks lifted from other, better movies. Slashed by dudes in masks.

Once he'd really told me why, his reason kind of shouldered mine out of the way. But Leona was not only not mad, at least not at the moment, but giggling like, Come on.

So I packed us a bowl and we tangled up together on the couch, chilly now, legs tucked under the comforter I'd taken off my bed, and we watched.

Scorpion Beach opens with a shot of a wreckage-strewn beach and Old Miami looming offshore, the crowns of buildings peeking through the surf break in a spectacular matte painting, out of which the girl gang comes tearing in pursuit of a speedboat. Smugglers. The gangs want their piece of the action or else. There's shots of different grinning, snarling women in gang gear on their Jet Skis, laughing, taunting. They gain on the speedboat and, like a killer-whale pack, surround and corral and force it onto the beach. The smugglers, two guys in overcoats even though it's clearly summer and hot as hell, take off running down the beach. Gang leader Julie Strain gives the order and the other girls dismount, and shots of bare feet in the sand are intercut with the smugglers in their suits and overcoats looking back all scared, and then the girls have them. Haul them back by their lapels and throw them like trophies at the feet of their leader, who's called Whiplash and wears a scorpion pendant dangling in the cleavage region. And in handing these smugglers over, Grandma Krista can be seen eyeing Julie Strain's throat, or, suggestively, the sweat-beaded region where the pendant is hanging, and she gets one of the movie's first real lines, asking Whiplash what she thinks they should do with these cheapskate scumbags.

"Dang," Leona said, sitting up. "She does look familiar."

"She was in some other stuff. A shark movie. An alien movie."

"Not that," she said, "I mean, look."

On-screen, Grandma Krista had one of the smugglers facedown in the sand with her foot on his back and her machine gun raised, while gang leader Julie Strain strutted around him, giving a speech that established who they were and what they were owed, even though this smuggler obviously knew all this already or else he wouldn't be in trouble, with his face all sandy and these vicious women looming over him.

Then Leona said, "She looks like you."

Cut to New Miami, where the streets were in a permanent shin-high flood through which the cop characters waded without apparent care for their shoes or clothes. Their vehicles were of the all-terrain and lifted sort, and their black knobby tires kicked up wake against the ragged warehouses of which, apparently, the entire future city was composed. The flooding of New Miami wasn't due to climate change, no, but the impact of an object from space, the remnant of an alien spacecraft or structure, no one could be sure, the true identity of the object buried in conspiracy and the subject of casual debate among the characters. For some of them, like Mike Hel, the detective, who was old enough to have experienced the event firsthand, the crash of this object was a massive and meaningful milestone, a moment which marked all the time around it. He could look out, as he did in the opening scene, over the wave-lapped ruins of Old Miami and see his own memories drowned. For the cultists who used a stolen fragment of this object to engender timeline chaos and to hasten the rule of their leader, Resnick, the impact was of religious significance. But for the generation that had grown up in the aftermath, like the members of the Jet Ski gang, the impact of the object buried out in the bay was history, a blameless fact around which their lives, like the waves around the sunken buildings, broke and ran on.

Pretty soon we weren't really watching anymore. It was more like we were in the presence of the film, set before it like you might sit before a fire. I was feeling the confluence of all the fucked-up things flowing through me, seeing the guy shot on the beach, Sheriff Laval's face, Rodney's, thinking about the party at the Yarbrough compound, where me and him were headed any day now.

"I don't want to go see those assholes celebrate," I said.

"Then don't," Leona said. "Stay here with me."

A little later Leona was shaking me awake, whispering to look. I thought Rodney had come home but it was just the movie, a part she wanted me to see. The girl gang from Scorpion Beach had the cop up against a graffiti-strewn wall, and half of them wanted to splatter him all over the place and the other half wanted to hear him out, if not believe him. The ones who wanted to listen were led by Julie Strain, and the ones who wanted him dead were spoken for by Grandma Krista, who jammed the nose of her machine gun into the cop's cheek and said how maybe it was time they decided who was gonna run this gang. The scene would end without bloodshed, one of the few such in *Scorpion Beach*, but there was a tension established between them that anybody, even two dumb kids high as hell thirty-something years later, could see would blossom into a final confrontation. Sure enough, it came right at the third-act turn, when Grandma Krista and Julie Strain's Whiplash squared off in the sand in a Rambo-knife-versus-bullwhip showdown that saw bikini straps slashed and perfect lines of blood in the corners of mouths and Grandma Krista lying there dying, making Whiplash promise not to lose her sting. For now, we knotted up together under the blanket in the last peace we'd know for a good long time, waiting to see what happened next.

CHAPTER FIVE

SHADOWFUCKING

"**B**elieve it or not," Rodney was saying, "we used to hate it here."

We, meaning him and his brother and their technical niece Destiny. "Here" could mean the house of slaughter we were parked in front of, or it could mean West Florida, which really meant Florida, because everybody hates Florida, apparently. That day of the passage of the bill, we were on our way to the party at Garcon Point and consequently he had the Governor and the massacre she'd saved him from on his mind, even though the day of solemn remembrance wasn't for another two months, because the way to the party took us past Tiger Cove. So he'd whipped us off the highway and past the guardhouse and through the back nine until we came to their street and their block and the house where it happened.

We sat in his truck, all dressed up for the party. Rodney in a black cotton blazer, an expensive red V-neck tee underneath, and on his hip a pistol in a snap holster, but not his whole gun rig. That morning I'd gone into the storage box in my bedroom closet and come out with a pair of the vintage West Florida polos from Pawpaw's era, like the one Rodney had worn when they came and got me. I brought them to Rodney in the morning with what I thought was a good attitude, like, Let's do this party but let's do it together. Let's show them what this family's got. Our West Florida.

He looked at the osprey shirts, crisp and folded in my arms.

He said I could wear that if I wanted but, you know what, he was good.

I tucked the shirts under my arm and acted like my heart wasn't breaking and I just went to my room. I was gonna text Leona but she'd already sent about ten messages asking what the fuck had I done and did I know what I'd done and saying that I needed to get over there NOW.

This was regarding the wasting of Buddy the cow and other things she'd stashed in their deep freezer, which I'd accidentally unplugged when I was helping out there over the weekend.

Four hours and a long hot shower later, I ended up in my only clean pair of jeans and a big white linen button-up from Nautica, a pair of aviators with orange mirror lenses in my collar. What I didn't wear was a pistol, even though Rodney offered and suggested and, on our way out the door, asked if I was sure.

"I got you with me, right?" I said, and he looked at me for the first time that day like, Yeah, you got me.

Maybe that's why he brought us to the murderhouse beforehand. He was feeling momentous and I had to act like I was too, even though I'd been here before. And not just as a baby. Now it was my turn to hurt his feelings, potentially.

"Hated it," he said, shaking his head at this place which, despite having changed since he lived there, must've still been beautiful to him, the way he said it.

"Even her?" I said.

"Especially her."

This was before it was a thing to hate Florida, or West Florida for that matter. And the Woolsack kids couldn't stand it. Were ashamed to find themselves there, even more ashamed to be thought of as having come from there, as opposed to Louisiana, their true ancestral home. Hated the people, who had come from everywhere, their voices snipping at consonants or drawn out in put-on drawls, Navy brats, Rust Belt fuckers, eastern exiles, shitheads from Louisiana, like them, who'd beef up their accents in order to define themselves against this pastel strip mall wasteland, but also those who gave up, lost their voices, blended in: it didn't matter. The place was fake as hell, they said, particularly as they edged into their teenage years and became living engines of hatred. They hated the beaches and the tourists who flocked to them, the clogged roads each summer and the cars with the "Local" bumper stickers, as if that was something to be proud of. Hated the weather, a weak-ass reflection of the real deep Louisiana heat, which these weak-ass people nonetheless complained about. Hated the pathetic version of Mardi Gras the place put on. Hated the food, mild on their spiteful tongues. Hated the music, a particular nightmare. Jimmy Buffett. Lynyrd Skynyrd. Twang and cocksure laziness. All in all, these children, each of whom had been born in that state, such as it was, bore for it the kind of blind and unreserved hatred that Americans of a later era, who ruthlessly mocked Florida and its inhabitants—despite said haters living in Rustfuck, Ohio, or some slate-skied East Coast brickhole—and called out in comments for its destruction, could only aspire to match. Try though they might, the people of America, thumbing away at their devices, streaming hatred and contempt, couldn't for a single instant reach the shrieking pitch of rage that sang inside the Woolsack children whenever they considered the state they were in.

And for their hate they were hated in turn, because this country loves to hate.

Indeed, no small number of their neighbors yearned for some magnificent and comprehensive violence to come someday and erase the Woolsacks from the world, for they had long disrupted the peace and security of the cul-de-sac with their parties and their fights, which were almost indistinguishable. The neighbors bemoaned the Woolsacks' trashy lives, where conflict and celebration looped like tire marks left in the turnaround after shithead kids did donuts in the middle of the night. The morning after the massacre, the neighbors would awake to the sounds of sirens and, with mugs of coffee in their hands, see law enforcement converge on the Woolsacks' house, and from their golf carts that day or the next they'd see the cops' tailgating tents erected in the yard, and these neighbors, who hated Florida in their own way, would be filled with the kind of peace and assurance known only to the righteous. Because what happened to the Woolsacks wasn't some random attack, but payback from people the family had pissed off. This wasn't senseless violence, it wasn't something that could happen to them, it was premeditated and based on a long-term grievance. It was a terrible act of revenge for a historical wrong. It said that if you hated something hard enough, then powers beyond you likely hated it too.

Some of this I gathered from Rodney and some of this I inferred and the rest I'd already soaked up from the air when I went to Tiger Cove with Leona. Since Rodney had blown up at me about her and still seemed to nurse suspicions, I'd been spending more time over at Leona's place. Ate fried bologna with her grandma, met the horses they boarded and their guinea fowl and their cow, Buddy, who was due to get slaughtered the week of the party. I was feeding Buddy some old chalky baby carrots, his big wet tongue and smooth round cow teeth working around my hand, and I was thinking, You're gonna be dead in, like, a day.

"Are you gonna eat Buddy?" I said.

"Of course I'm gonna eat Buddy," she said, reaching to scratch between his ears. "Have you ever gone and looked at the house where your mom and them got killed?"

I stared at her. We had murdered moms in common so she thought she could bring it up whenever and I wouldn't be fazed. Now I was in fact fazed, but I didn't let her know it, except I was so busy staring I left my hand in Buddy's mouth, and he was so gentle he didn't even bite. Later I'd help load him into the trailer that would take him to the processor, and still later I'd waste all 1,425 USDA Premium Choice pounds of him.

"Hey," Leona said.

"No," I said, taking my hand away from Buddy. "I haven't gone and looked."

Unlike the old West Florida property out on Garcon Point, I hadn't asked Rodney to take me out to Tiger Cove. Partly because it was right there, like a mile at most up the road. I could've walked over there anytime I wanted, which is why I hadn't gone on my own, because if something has lived in your head for thirteen years, seeing it in real life can be kind of anticlimactic. The whole thing suddenly seems small, and you along with it. But I didn't say any of that to Leona, and she wanted to go, so we took her grandma's busted 4Runner and went to go and look.

We sat in the cab of the 4Runner with the engine going and both of us sweating even though the AC was on and the windows were up, staring at the house like we were the ones about to bust in. The house was on a corner lot, facing the sound and backing onto the twelfth-hole fairway. There was a live oak in the yard that'd taken one too many hurricanes. No moss in its boughs. Leaves an off shade. Then Leona said, "You think that fence is locked?"

"I don't know." I looked away.

"I think it's open. And the driveway's empty."

"OK. So?"

"So I don't think anybody's home," Leona said. "So I think we should go swim."

"I got a pool."

"I got a pool too," she said back. "But is your pool filled with legend? Is your pool a significant location in the history of West Florida?"

I said in point of fact my pool was filled with pine straw right now and looked like rusty tap water and she said Rusty Tapwater sounded like a bull rider or a race car driver, and we laughed about that for a minute until she got serious again, a kind of serious that didn't have to do with murdered moms but was still about life and death, and she said, "I want to go swim."

Well, she could've said she wanted to go start World War III and it wouldn't have mattered to me. I'd have gone to that water with her no matter what.

She left the truck running and off we went, across the yard, in broad daylight, which to a neighborhood like this might as well be blackest night because nobody was home, even housewives, and yard crews and grounds keepers don't give a shit about kids splashing around in a pool and whatever else they get up to behind closed, unlocked fences.

The backyard was all pool deck, that kind of concrete or whatever that looks like acne scars, all dusted with planting soil and white fertilizer nibs. Saggy loungers in a row and parked athwart them was one of those red plastic toddler cars you have to push with your feet. Lime trees in pots on cast-iron stands, fruit gone weird and spiky. Big old dog-poisoning sago palms and Spanish bayonet posted along the fence, guarding the pool noodles and toys that'd ended up there. Plastic diving rings and bubble wands and a faded Elsa kickboard.

We stripped down and dove in and floated, treading. Off in the shallows a vacuum robot was bumping around, trailing its cord. I wondered about the kids who lived here, their parents. What did it mean to them, the awful things that'd happened here, and what about the things to come? Their vehicles might've been covered in stickers declaring their feelings, but the lack of signage in the yard made me clock them as neutral or opposed to Troy Yarbrough's plan. They'd wake up tomorrow in his West Florida and then what? The mom and dad feeling edgy, tired after staying up late, talking things out. All their reassurances gone stale like morning breath. Then they'd see their little ones trailing rainbow bubbles or Flintstoning around in their chunky plastic car and they'd share a smile that meant, Yeah, the world is menacing and unpredictable but here we go, together.

"You really going to that party?" Leona said.

I said it wasn't that easy and she said she was pretty sure it was and I said, "I'm going for Rodney."

"But those people are fucking assholes," she said. "You don't have to go for him, or for whatever crazy homeless woman you think is gonna be the leader of your state or whatever."

"She's not homeless," I said. "She's rich."

Leona flung herself back into a dead man's float and with her eyes shut said, "Fine."

Considering this, it was strange as hell to be back here, sitting in the truck with Rodney, all done up for the party, having what's supposed to be a momentous staredown of the property where events occurred that shaped our lives all those years ago, and not be thinking about any of that.

I was thinking about Leona.

The way I was thinking about Leona made my face look tender, which Rodney mistook for us sharing a serious heartfelt moment, and because serious heartfelt moments are supposed to be rare between the kind of men who run around with guns, I felt bad, which had the unintended effect of bringing me back to the moment he wanted to share.

I said, "But did y'all hate West Florida too?"

"Definitely," he said. "Maybe even hated it worse because it wasn't real . . . to us. It was just some shit your Pawpaw made up."

Unlike Leona's grandma's truck, Rodney kept his fresh, and with the windows rolled up the truck smelled like nothing but Armor All wipes and gun oil, cordite, and, I guess, me, because at that moment he flared his nostrils and said, "You smell like blood. Why do you smell like blood?"

My hands went by instinct to my face and I sniffed and said I didn't smell anything. Truth was I'd been arm-deep in cow's blood and meat that day, which was the second thing Leona was pissed at me about, other than going to the party.

Since we were sharing a moment I decided to tell him what had happened.

It wasn't like I'd killed anybody, anyway.

It was Buddy. I'd helped Leona load him into the trailer, seen him off to slaughter. But I wasn't there when he returned in 124 individually wrapped packs, which Leona and her grandma loaded into their freezers out in the toolshed. I didn't see her again for a couple days, and I could tell she was mad because of the party, so I walked over unannounced. Leona wasn't there, so I asked her grandma if there was any work around the place I could do. There was and I did, but what I didn't do is remember that the same extension cord I was running the band saw through attached to the shed with the twin Deepfreezes, where Buddy and other items were in cold storage. I left, feeling tired but accomplished, and when I talked to Leona that night it was like everything was fine again, but the next day she came screaming down the beach. I'd unplugged the freezers and now there was a thousand pounds of rotten stinking meat to get rid of.

"And you cleaned all that shit up?"

"Yeah."

Rodney shook his head in a the-things-we-do-for-love sense.

I summoned up my courage and asked him, "Who is she?"

"Who's who?"

"You know," I said.

He slowed the truck and pulled over to the curb and leaned against the wheel. "It's complicated," he said.

"How complicated?"

He looked at me hard. "Very. Fucking. Complicated," he said. "But you just be patient and you'll find out soon enough."

I kept my mouth shut as we wove through the narrow streets of the development on the shores of Santa Rosa Sound, watching the clouds unfurl their vapors in the last of the twilight.

In the yards we saw signs, mostly red signs bearing the hashtag #BestFlorida and the occasional sadder #OneFlorida signs in the yards of, like, professors and people who couldn't admit they were outnumbered, outgunned, and who weren't crazy enough to stand up to crazy people and meet them at a pitch of madness that could come close to evening the odds.

I watched the signs flit past, staked in yards that would be battlefields soon. Then we merged onto 281 and the Garcon Point Bridge, riding to the other side of the water.

I said, "I still think Go West is a better, like, tagline."

"Agreed," he said. "But I'd be lying, and I think you'd be lying too, if I didn't say I was a little bit excited about this whole thing."

"West Florida's us," I said. "Our family. Not this Jesus shit."

"Jesus is where the money is, man. Plus, you don't think they actually believe that shit, do you?"

"Some of 'em do."

"Not all of 'em," he said. "Don't be so uptight about it. The whole thing's just shadowfucking anyway. No big deal."

"Shadow what?"

"Shadowfucking. It's what your Pawpaw would say about events and shit. The public stuff you do so you can make real deals in private. You gotta do it, the parties and the dinners and all that, but they feel about as good as fucking a shadow."

"Then what am I supposed to be excited about, again?"

"I don't know, maybe you could find it in yourself to get excited about meeting, say, Riley Rae?"

"Yeah right," I said.

"Bullshit."

"Nah," I shook my head.

"I say again, bullshit. I refuse to believe you're so hung up on old four-wheeler cow's blood back there down on the farm that you can't get a little jazzed about meeting someone who is literally famous for being hot."

"First of all, she's famous for being fucked up and liking fucked-up shit."

"Well," he said, wagging his head, "then she's gonna love your ass, isn't she."

In truth, Riley Rae Yarbrough was famous for several reasons, both locally and beyond. When she was a teenager she'd

been on *Redneck Riviera* on TLC, where the hook was that her
dad was this Florida politician and her mom ran a megachurch
Christian college, so her escapades and impromptu concerts
and staged girl-kissing were supposed to be transgressive. I'd
watched the show with Amber because it ran before *The Real
Housewives of NOLA*, and even the Dakotas would show up,
because they thought Riley Rae was super hot in a wounded,
messy, self-destructive way that made them feel like they could
pounce on her. So did Big Mike, which always made everybody
uncomfortable when he'd walk by the couch on his way to
the garage or whatever and be like, Mmmmmmm. Even the
Dakotas shuddered at that. But all of us sat up straight and
paid attention whenever Riley Rae burst into song. Which was
often, because it was her thing, and on shows like that each
person has to do their thing at least twice per season.

Then Aunt Amber died and I didn't catch season five of
Redneck Riviera, in the middle of which Riley Rae had a break-
down and was hospitalized and subsequently retreated from
the public eye. Rumor was drugs, depression, bipolar disorder.
I recall some that said she'd gotten pregnant but hadn't known
until these stomach pains started and when she finally went to
the hospital they scanned her and found the baby but it was
dead, long dead, like since she was way younger dead, and back
when it got formed and died it was just the size of a Cheeto
Puff but over the years it had been mineralized, transformed,
so that when they cut it out at West Florida Regional Surgical
Center the long-gone baby was now a crystal egg.

A tech had snapped a picture of the egg before, he said, some people wrapped it up and took it away, and people in videos commented on the picture and judged it authentic, and many others said so too.

A year or so later, around the time her dad, State Rep. Troy Yarbrough, switched from dogging on trans kids to talking about West Florida, she'd found herself again. Now her dad had stolen our family's idea and put a Christian spin on it and she'd reemerged, reborn, a viral sensation making these videos where she came out in wild costumes singing about the Great State of West Florida. Her dad's West Florida. Ours was just some See Also at the bottom of the wiki page shit.

"I mean come on," Rodney said, still doubting my lack of excitement. "She looks like one of the characters from that anime you like."

"Sounds like you're the one who's excited, honestly."

He grinned. "You know I don't fuck with them young girls."

"Mommies only," I said, and then was sorry I said it when I saw Rodney's face.

We'd come off the bridge and were working now through the developments north of the state forest on Garcon Point. I could almost hear what he said in the edges of the words he'd actually used. That was the thing with Rodney, he was better in a ton of ways, truly, than somebody like Big Mike, but you could tell there was a Big Mike beneath the surface, just waiting to come out.

Maybe that's true of all guys his age. Or, worse, all of us in general.

I was smarting even though you had to admit that was true. Riley Rae did look like that now. Gone was the version of her from *Redneck Riviera* with bleach-streaked highlit hair, the messy buns, the fishtails. The party-girl cutoffs and designer tanks. Here came neon-red dye and hip-length extensions in twin tails and the armored-looking sailor suits with the red wolf on the chest. Even when there wasn't a filter on, when someone else was filming, Riley Rae looked far from real. But that wasn't the hard part to admit. The hard part was that she *did* look like the kind of character I, well . . . The more I thought about it the more Riley Rae started making Leona look small and scruffy by comparison.

I didn't want to admit that, so I decided to fuck with Rodney instead.

"So you don't think the Troy Yarbrough guy is a dick anymore."

"I never said that."

"You said worse, Mister Shadowfucker."

"Well, maybe let's don't repeat that at this party, then, shall we?"

"I'm just saying. Like, you told me the guy was crazy."

"Look," he said, his voice suddenly getting all confidential, like he knew something I didn't. "We don't need to worry about Troy, OK?"

I thought about the Troy Yarbrough I'd seen in clips and posts. I thought about the dolphin and what Leona said and the state senator falling, shot in the eye. Troy Yarbrough and whoever was with him seemed more than a little worrisome to me, but that wasn't how Rodney was feeling.

"Don't ask me how," he said, "but trust me, Troy's not gonna be our problem long."

"Why?"

Rodney sliced a glare at me.

"You said not to ask how."

"Ask a different question."

"If this isn't you going to bend a knee to Troy Yarbough, then why *are* we going?"

"Because it's time we got with the fucking program, you know?"

"What program?"

"Jesus Christ," he said. "Look, I was the one who didn't want to deal with them. I was the one saying no, I didn't want to go sit down with Troy. Then I thought about it and I thought about it and I figured, this is for real. It's gonna change everything, and we can either be a part of it or we can get left behind."

"It wasn't real before?"

"That's different," he said, squinting into the sunset. "That's family."

I thought about that as he drove us through the last of the subdivisions. It was one thing for your crazy-ass, impossible family to be into the idea and another for the idea to be taken by some other, possibly crazy-ass people who weren't yours at all and for them to have it all official and ready for a vote, with everything on their terms.

Rodney shook his head and we came to the land that should've been ours. A wide entrance fronted with a sign of stainless steel inlaid with gold that said WEST FLORIDA ESTATES.

We passed boys in fresh-pressed tactical uniforms on camo UTVs and approached a gated entrance.

"What do you think the Governor's gonna think? When she comes back."

"She can think whatever she wants."

Traitor, I wanted to say.

Liar, I wanted to say even more.

Rodney rolled his window down and flashed a card at a key reader, and the gate slid open and we went on up a drive lined with little gem magnolias planted in 1992, one of the things Pawpaw had gotten done before he had to sell it all, and followed the drive to where it looped before the house.

I didn't ask him where he'd gotten the card. I was too busy gaping at what could have been ours.

The house was based on the Old Governor's Mansion from back in Louisiana, the one built by Huey P. Long that was supposedly based on the White House as originally envisioned by Thomas Jefferson. It was a stately hulk of Georgian architecture, raised twenty feet off the ground on terraced limestone steps, only it was painted the palest coral pink. While I gawked at the house, Rodney steered us past the driveway loop, where he said no thanks to the valet, who then pointed us towards some kids in orange vests with light sticks who directed us into a gravel side lot, where we parked behind some Lincoln SUVs with their drivers still in them and a whole row of Escambia County and Santa Rosa County cruisers.

I pointed to a pale-green cruiser marked Santa Rosa County Sheriff's Department. "Claudia's, you think?"

"More like her dad's," he said. "Anyway, don't worry about her. Worry about what you're gonna say to Riley Rae and how you're gonna explain it all to your girl."

Coming around the eastern edge of the house, you could feel the music pulsing, the celebration underway. The yard and side paths were filled with caterers carrying plastic bins and pushing handcarts, and we were met by Trip, executive assistant to Troy Yarbrough, who said hello to Rodney and that he was so glad to see him again.

Again? I wanted to ask but didn't because Trip was shaking my hand and asking my name.

Rodney leaned in: "His name's—"

"—Murderbaby," I said, thinking I was being cute.

Trip didn't even blink, just smiled and thanked me and said that was quite the moniker. Explained, as he walked us through a hedge of hawthorn into the party, that his name was a nickname too, Trip because he was the third person to bear his actual name. I had the sense that, despite being Whatever the Third, Trip here had seen some shit.

I thought I'd seen some shit in my day too, but I was awed at the size of this whole affair. The backyard, if you could call it that, was an enormous lawn that spread down to the water's edge, set with white tents with plastic windows and water misters and fans, and at the center of the yard an enormous pool deck grew from the rear portico of the house, which unlike the front was a peristyle, with limestone steps maybe eight feet high. The pool deck was arranged with gleaming white furniture and drink stations and people arranged in various upbeat poses. I didn't notice the security until Rodney pointed them out. Pairs of guys in polos and aviators and chest plate armor flexing in their interview stances. One-hour shifts at each station. Two in the backyard. Two in the front by the steps with the valets. Hands locked on their duty belts, standing there looking badass.

Amidst the partygoers went young men in a mishmash of modern tactical and colonial uniforms, shirts with leather drawstrings at their collars, plate-carrier vests, tricorn hats, sabers at their sides in polished-brass parade scabbards, and AR-15s hanging from their shoulders by leather straps. You'd see them milling around the trunks of palms, or gathered on a strip of lawn that led down to a brilliant half-moon of white sand that opened onto the bay and the lights of the city beyond.

They had a kind of menace in their eyes I hadn't seen since the Dakotas squared off with Rodney at the airstrip. One look at them and you'd think their bill hadn't passed at all.

The music was whomping and I smelled cordite on the air from displays of hissing sparklers. There was no serious dancing yet, but people were light and loose, gripping their drinks as if those sweaty plastic-crystal tumblers were anchors holding them to earth. They'd won, and now anything was possible. Not that these seemed like the kind of people who weren't used to winning. But still.

The youngest people were girls decked in gold and diamond hardware, older teenagers and twentysomethings who moved halfheartedly to the music or arrayed themselves on furniture about the pool deck in states of fixed and silent judgment or took pictures of themselves, lips pursed.

I didn't see Sheriff Laval anywhere. Or Claudia.

The rest of the partygoers were older couples, the owners of local businesses, officeholders, lawyers. Some had come straight from Tallahassee by private jet the moment the votes had been secured, hours before the bill officially passed. Rodney didn't pay much mind to the men, some of whom acted like they knew him from videos or whatever, but he did linger on their wives. You could tell he was interested even if you didn't know Rodney the way I knew him. This was the man who told me once when he was very high and briefly happy that he loved sun lines on the chests of ladies here in their forties, fifties, not to mention freckles, and for as long as he could remember he'd wanted to put his lips right there. Mouth to sternum. He also confessed to me that night that he liked sucking on wet swimsuits, and that night or some other he recalled to me how, when he was maybe seven, one of Grandma Krista's friends from the assessor's office, the office manager Irene, the spitting image of *Star Trek: TNG*'s Deanna Troi, came to the house in Tiger Cove so her boyfriend could watch some sports event on the big screen with Alexis's boyfriend at the time. While the boyfriends stayed inside and hollered at the screen, the rest of them went out to the pool and swam, which ended up somehow with Irene squishing him against her and him trying to breathe with his mouth on the wet one-piece. He'd been chasing that sensation basically ever since.

You live with a guy, you learn all this shit. Or you think you do.

That same night, I told him about Braiden Cartier, and he didn't even sit up, he just reached over from where he was lying on the couch and touched my arm and said it was OK. Just like Leona or Riley Rae or some random bot friending me on Instagram were exceptions to the Braiden Cartier rule of my attractions, I guess Claudia was the exception to Rodney's, in terms of age. On this basis, I thought we understood each other, but there was still plenty that I didn't know, and he kept things buried down so deep I guess he would've never told me unless he had to.

Trip led us around to the head of the pool, where we stood before the party's centerpiece. Set on a marble pediment

at the foot of the steps that led down from the house, an ice
sculpture depicted a red wolf and what appeared to be an
osprey, lit from within by LEDs that shone through electric
blue and red, like there were small police first responders
inside it. Guests milled around the sculpture, drinks in their
hands, the mist thrown off the ice wafting around their heads,
and none of them approached us where we stood. Rodney
faced the sculpture and the house above it and Trip, who
stood beside the sculpture, pointing out details, commenting
on the craftsmanship and the challenges of carving two kinds
of North American predators at quadruple scale out of ice,
much less keeping that ice sharp and clear and free of melt.

"Nice," Rodney said, and he nodded to me where I was
standing off to the side, like I was supposed to say "Nice," too.

So I did. Not that Rodney noticed. He was plainly too
caught up in it all, and I didn't even know the half of how
caught up he was yet. How caught up we all were.

"We hoped you'd like it," Trip said. "It's a tribute," he
went on, his voice going as sharp and cold as the sculptures,
"to your late father's legacy."

While I eased closer to the ice to feel the cool mist on
my face, Trip was giving an admiring paraphrase of Pawpaw's
words on the osprey, how the osprey was a real inspiration
to Mr. Yarbrough, even though of course they'd chosen their
own emblem, the wolf.

Then Trip started into the red wolf's rebirth and how, if
we wanted, we could go later and see the kennels where the

first litters had been born, and Rodney was nodding like an asshole at the righteousness of this as Trip went on until his eyes cut over Rodney's shoulder for a second and he stumbled. I followed his gaze to see a woman in a wide red straw hat walking towards us through the crowd. I watched her approach and took note of the twitch in Trip's lip as he tried to conceal from Rodney the fact that he was watching her come up, too. We both acted like we weren't seeing what was coming until the woman stood right behind him, a half head taller. Mostly I saw the hat, an enormous Eric Javits Squishee the saturated color of old movie gore, the floppy brim so broad it shaded her bare shoulders and cast her face in darkness.

"Ma'am," Trip said, and Rodney finally turned. I knew it right then, could see it plain as day in his eyes when he saw her.

Rachael Kingdom Yarbrough.

President of Emerald Coast Christian College.

Potential First Lady of the new West Florida.

Wife of Troy Yarbrough, whose appearance we were all supposedly eagerly awaiting.

Rodney's mouth was working into a smile and his head got this fake-ass wobble of surprise, like, Oh, who's this now? Caught between them, Trip was trying to appear serene.

Rachael Kingdom tilted her head back so the brim of her hat formed a kind of halo behind her, and she said to Rodney, "We're so glad you're finally with us again."

Poor Trip looked like he was ready to fall out, and I was rolling the hell out of my eyes, not just to be a teenage shit but because I was starting to understand the depth of what Rodney had kept from me. There was nothing else I could do to convey how betrayed I felt, but I didn't have a chance to be ruder to her because what Rachael Kingdom did next snapped my eyes back in place such that I haven't rolled them fuckers since.

What she did was slightly bend, because, it's true, I'm shorter than Rodney, but everybody there was shorter than her. Rachael Kingdom bent in such a way that her shoulders rolled forward and, somehow, instead of making her shorter, it was as if this posture, the posture of talking to a little child, endowed her with an even greater height, and I can't recall if her hands were on her knees but it felt like they were, and she said to me, "And you, aren't you something."

Rodney flinched and I was a bottle of thin glass suddenly filled with questions, most of which I'd never get to ask. I couldn't speak, and without even time enough to judge my own feelings, in that moment there erupted from the house the loud clear notes of whipstroke synth.

One half of the tall French doors had opened, and out strode a man in dress clothes with his shirt collar unbuttoned and pulled down by the weight of a pair of black sunglasses framed in gold, his sleeves rolled high as ever. Troy Yarbrough. His arms were leathery and thin and veins stood out all over him like he was fixing to explode through the sheer pressure of whatever coursed inside him. It seemed impossible but he looked thinner in person, like even more of a suntanned ghoul. He wore no tie or sidearm and he was barefoot, pant legs rolled to the taper of his calf as if he'd just been wading in shallow water.

Trip was clapping, and all around us the other guests had turned from where Rodney and I stood with Rachael and were clapping too. We were twenty, thirty yards away, max. Hard to think we hadn't been positioned here to give us just this very view, of the eagle and the steps and the man himself on the portico directly above. Meanwhile, the boys in tactical/colonial uniforms had mounted the steps and now stood ranked on either side of Troy, holding the muzzles of their machine guns in parade rest. Behind him, off to the side of the colonnade, stood a man I took to be his bodyguard, a big bearded bastard whose arms were bursting out of his red wolf tee and absolutely crawling with tattoos. He wore wraparound shades but I didn't need to see his eyes to know he was looking at us all like either he wanted us dead or we were already dead and gross, rotting, shambling in place before him.

Soon the music and the clapping stopped, and when the last stray yeahs and whoops and squeals had gone up in the air and ceased, Troy Yarbrough began to speak.

"Ladies and gentleman," he said to scattered cheers, whistles.

"West Floridians," he said, and my ears honestly hurt for the force of their roar. I didn't think these types had it in them, but here they were, bellowing like it was a ballgame. Glancing around, I saw the loudest were Troy's boys in uniform. Jacked-up human amplifiers, their eyes fixed on him.

"On the day of this great victory," Troy went on, when they quieted down. "A day that will be remembered in the annals of this state—*our* state—we're gonna have a whole lot of people to thank, and a whole lot of celebrating to do. But I want to make something clear to you about the future here. I want to let you know that I have heard you, we have heard you. And we are tired of the mad." He paused, raised his chin. "We are sick and tired of the mad. There isn't a single person here whose life has not been touched by madness. The madness of the secular; the madness of class war; the madness of perceived wrongs; the madness of the mutilation of children; the madness of race; the madness of gender; the madness that lives behind the eyes of the people you love, who you trust until they . . . they . . ."

Rachael Yarbrough had eased closer to Rodney and the enormous red corona of her Squishee hat was blocking my view. I stepped around her a little, saw the veins in Troy's temples pumping even though he wasn't shouting, wasn't angry, yet. He'd trailed off but quickly caught himself, and now he spoke in a strong, calm voice, explaining how madness can erupt from those we trust, how our country, the state that claims to be ours has abandoned us to the raving hordes of the totally insane.

"The mad wander our streets, shoot up our schools, burn through our money for which we get what? More madmen on the streets. More massacres in schools. More mutilations. More betrayals. You can lie down beside someone for a lifetime and the next day pull back the sheet and what's there but a writhing mass of snakes. But not anymore. Not us and not here, because in the great state of West Florida we will have a way.

"We will have a way for the parent, who sees their son on the verge of violence, to get that son the help he needs and to keep all our children safe. We will have a way for the homeowner, who sees his property defiled, his peace shattered each day, to make his home and peace inviolate.

"We will create, in this state, a system of Houses of Recovery and Resource, so these people can get the help they need, modeled after the Faith Houses created by my beloved wife, Rachael Kingdom, through Emerald Coast Christian College, where for twenty years, struggling young women have gone for comfort and restoration. She's right here, I see her. Give her a hand."

Rachael Kingdom gracefully raised a freckle-spattered forearm. Gave a queenly wave. I thought about my mom, about what kind of young women in what kind of struggles ended up in a place like that. I thought either I was going to vomit or I might burn this whole place to the goddamn ground.

"We will empower our police, we will empower our citizens and invest them with the authority to say, 'No, this maniac who smells like human waste should not be on the corner of my street, yelling.' To say, 'No, this child saying he is a girl when he is a boy should not be allowed to carve himself apart.' To say, 'No, they need to go away.' We will have these houses in every city, in every county across West Florida, and by the end of the first year of our state's existence, we will know greater peace than we could've ever dreamed."

When the applause died down, Troy raised one wooden-looking hand and led the guests in a pledge.

"Hail the flag of West Florida; I pledge allegiance to thee, with reverence and devotion to the land of freedom which it . . . re-represents, one state, under God, whole and ir- . . . ir- . . ."

At first, when he started choking again on his words, the voices of the forgathered had risen awkwardly with Troy's, some stumbling, others laughing awkwardly, looking at each other like, You seeing this? but as he stumbled his boys in the crowd took the lead, speaking the rest with force until the others joined in, too. Meanwhile, Troy Yarbrough was shaking, as if the remaining words of the pledge had lodged themselves deep in his chest and he was trying to urge them out. His throat rippled and bobbed and he was staring out at the crowd, almost pleading. Like his insides had been scooped out and blended and poured back into him, and he wanted to know who'd done this awful thing.

At some unseen signal, about ten of his uniformed boys came and formed two lines and drew their rifles and shoul-dered them and made a tunnel behind Troy, who was stock-still like his feet were nailed to the ground, until the tattooed body-guard slipped out of the colonnade and took Troy Yarbrough by the elbow and led him away as the music burst once more from the speakers.

I elbowed Rodney and he folded his arms and looked at me like, Told you so, nothing to worry about with this motherfucker. Rachael Kingdom stood beside him impassive as the guests' heads began to bob, looks of recognition and disbelief fading as their shoulders began to roll and the speakers erupted into slicing urgent synthesized violin, and then they were all of them dancing, hands in the air, phone screens endlessly repeating this scene.

And out of the tunnel of muskets came Riley Rae, a sequined red wolf howling on her chest, jaws spread and glittering from the halter collar of her leotard down to the claws that dug into her stomach as she pumped her knees at center stage and marched out to face the crowd and the music soared and she began to sing.

It was a massive electronic bubblegum triumph, and Riley Rae sang the hell out of it, I must admit. One hand cradling the mic close, the other sweeping out over the crowd. You could about see the souls lifting out of some of them when she tapped her finger on the air above their heads. The kind of song that starts when the end credits are about to roll and the title card slams onscreen one last time. In front of me, the sunset of Rachael Kingdom's hat was rocking back and forth. I figured she had probably written the song herself. In fact it was lifted, pretty much straight, with a few changes to the lyrics, from a show that'd played long before I was born, in which a young girl singer helped humankind win an intergalactic war against gigantic aliens who had neither sex nor love nor, crucially, music. The girl would sing her battle hymn as fleets of spaceships laced each other with beams of energy, and the aliens in their green lumpy alien ships would be dazzled by the song and by outnumbered, outgunned humanity's gumption, giving enough time for Earth's transforming fighter jets to send spiraling missiles into their gross lumpy alien hulls.

Rodney told me about it later, on the ride home, when I was texting Leona and feeling shitty so I picked on the song Riley Rae had sung. That was Rachael Kingdom's song, really, he told me. Back in the eighties, her parents, June and Anson, had banned her from watching anything so worldly, what with the pop music and the presence of alien life contradicting scripture. So she'd snuck episodes in secret, bought the tapes through friends. She'd even shown him an episode or two back when she babysat him and the show was in syndication.

While her daughter hit the last verse, Rachael Kingdom gave Rodney's arm a quick squeeze that I couldn't have been the only person to see, and then she slipped away.

I didn't understand it then and maybe I don't now, but standing there when Riley Rae truck a pose with her mic upheld like the Statue of Liberty with her sword aimed at the sky, ordaining a knife-point freedom on us all, I had the feeling I was living someone else's dream.

I was caught in the storm of their elation, dying to get out. All I could do was think of Leona and tell myself I'd be back there with her soon.

They kept us there until way late. I didn't realize when it was happening, but that's what they were doing. Night came on and sparklers appeared and were dispersed among the guests and whenever Trip found us, he introduced us to more guests, some of whom claimed to have known Pawpaw.

He sure was something, they'd say. No one like him. One of a kind.

These men had known RJ Woolsack when he was buying property here. They seemed to think me and Rodney should be just so glad that, if things had to work out this way, at least the property, the whole West Florida thing, went to the right hands.

God's will, they said. Things work out the way they're supposed to, don't they?

"They sure do," Rodney said, eyes narrowing.

The old men who wanted to talk about Pawpaw were bad enough, but worse were the ones who wanted to tell him about Grandma Krista. Miss Hawaiian Tropic Pensacola Beach. The whole thing. Rodney would manage a grunt, finger his rodeo ring, scanning the periphery of wherever we happened to be standing. I'd just be wondering how anybody could have so much money that they'd think it was fine to annoy someone standing here with a pistol on his hip who'd fought at least fifteen gunfights.

While these oblivious oldsters kept a cordon of awkwardness around him, I'd make little forays off into the pool deck and the property. The pool ran fifty-something yards and ended with the lawn that flowed down, eastward, to the slip and the launch and the boathouse whose roof I could see in the light of the torches staked in the yard. Trip had taken us down to the boathouse earlier, to witness the fleet of Jet Skis and cabin cruisers and Carolina Skiffs and, yes, the black speedboat Leona had seen. I'd said, Cool, and Rodney had said, Cool, or something equally appropriate, but he'd looked at it the way he'd looked at everything here: like he was searching his memory for what it had been, and was faced with what it was, the idea of what it could've been.

On my little jaunts away from the diminishing crowd, I'd go out to the edge of the deck and look around, pull a Gulf Lite from a nearby bucket and sip and read my phone. I drank the beer way too fast and studied the inland portions of the property. To the west the lawn faded and the yard was hulked with outbuildings whose shapes were less visible, their purposes less apparent. The edge of the neighborhood, the settlement that never was.

Trip kept bringing people by and I kept going out to that lip of concrete by myself, but there was a moment when Rodney and I were briefly left alone. The party was winding down, and you could hear the engines revving in the grass lot and in the drive and people's voices saying bye. Rodney caught a crick or something because he had his hands on his hips and was stretching, yawning, nodding as he did, like he was taking all this in.

"It would've been crazy," I said, "if this was ours."

"Yeah," Rodney said. "Crazy's right."

"You ever wonder what you would've been? Like what if Pawpaw had kept it, what if everything had worked out?"

His face jerked into a scowl and he said, "What if there had been an earthquake? What if it rains tomorrow? 'What if' don't mean shit."

My voice got small and I said, "OK."

"Anyway," he said, voice gone low, "we're here now."

Just past midnight, I texted Leona and she said, You're still there? and I said, Yeah but not for long, because when I looked back the pool deck was basically empty except for one group sitting around a fire pit and another further up towards the house, where I'd left Rodney. Out on the lawn the caterers were buttoning the windows of the tents and you could hear the pop of garbage bags like sails filling with a high wind.

I told Leona I'd seen the black boat and she said, Eww, and laughed and I sent her some dumbshit GIF back, and when I put the phone in my pocket and started back towards the house I honestly felt like everything was OK and in a little while hopefully I'd be back in the truck with Rodney and we'd be heading home and it would all go back to normal.

On my way, I passed the fire pit group and even though I was wobbly from the beer I almost jumped when I saw it was Riley Rae, no longer in costume, seated on a rattan sofa, holding court with some of her friends in a circle of matching furniture situated around a low brazier of polished metal that gave off a big blue holographic-looking flame.

Then one by one they stopped talking—Riley Rae first, the rest buttoning up in turn—and watched in silence as I went by. I know that kind of silence when you're walking by and what it means when it comes from a group of people like that. I can read such things the way some people can read clouds and say, We better pack up 'cuz it looks like rain. What that silence means is that a burst of laughter's coming. I felt a familiar tightness between my shoulder blades and running down to my tailbone.

But no matter how far away I went, no laughter came. No voices, no sounds at all. Or maybe they did but by then I was too far away and too astonished to notice, because I'd come up on the group around Rodney and had seen who was there.

Troy Yarbrough, for one, seeming somewhat restored from his attack earlier. I tried to edge away from him, out of his range, but I didn't have to worry about that. All his focus was on Rodney anyway. Beside Troy Yarbrough stood the tatted guard, watching him like he was about to explode in a hail of bone, like we were the ones who needed protection from him.

"I heard about what happened to you and your family," the tattooed man said to Rodney. "I'm sorry about that."

Rodney was showing his canines. "It was a long time ago."

"The Electrician here is a master shot," said Troy, putting a hand to the shoulder of his man. "Even if he's too doggone modest to say."

The man in question said nothing at all.

"Nice," Rodney said. "You ever go on DU3L?"

The Electrician raised his chin. "I quit playing with guns when I was little."

"You do what, then? Wiring?"

"Sometimes. I'm a contractor. I don't work without getting paid. It's no game for me."

"Shame," Rodney said. "I think I'd like to see your draw."

"Yeah?" The Electrician waited a moment. "You serve?"

"Serve what?"

The Electrician snorted.

"I take it you saw some action, spreading freedom?" Rodney said, and even Troy Yarbrough's insane ass was looking uncomfortable.

The Electrician blinked slow. "Nobody likes being asked that," he said flatly.

"No shit? I got stabbed a couple dozen times and my whole family got killed and people always ask my ass about it. So what'd you do when you got out? Get you a dog to hug on when there's fireworks?"

Their eyes were locked and you could see the slack run through Rodney from his right shoulder on down, like secret linkages were uncoupling, the way he'd limber up before a gunfight, knees flexing into his stance. Me, I was wound all tight and tighter still seeing Troy Yarbrough's eyes widen and his mouth open, urging. I thought they were about to throw down when Troy clapped his hands and said, "Come on. A couple shots before y'all go, how about it?"

You'd have thought he was talking about bourbon, Troy said it so easy, but then he had his hands on both of them and led them out into the dark and I followed. For the next few minutes the two of them laid down fire on the reflectors of traffic barrels in a contest I didn't quite see because, like I told Rodney I was going to do when they were hauling the barrels up, I waited at the truck. Ours was pretty much the only vehicle left in the grass lot so I could see straight out into the yard where they'd lined the barrels up, could see their muzzle flashes and the gunsmoke and the flicker of the fire beyond them on the pool deck.

I took my phone out, told Leona we were on our way.

You said that an hour ago, she said.

I told her yeah but Rodney had to do some shooting and she said of course he did. I was trying but then she said, honestly, she hoped Rodney killed all these motherfuckers, and I said, I think he wants to, pretty much. Except for one, but I didn't tell her that. She said, lol I hope you survive, and I hearted that. I leaned back in the seat, watched the stars paint the windshield. I was waiting at the truck because I didn't want my eardrums blown out, but the roar of gunfire as they emptied each of their pieces was still damn near deafening, so that when Rodney finally came to the car and I said hey, he didn't hear me and I couldn't tell what he was saying, if he was saying anything at all.

"Well," I said when we were in gear, "did you win?"

"Motherfucker's a good shot." Rodney popped the brights on, stared at the road. It was late as hell and pitch black on the shell road that led out of the property. "Different when it's for real, though, and this wasn't for fucking real."

"It was really fucking sucky is what it was. That song? I mean, come on."

"Sucky?" he said. "How 'bout you sucky on some quiet for a sec."

"I've been quiet."

"Be quiet more."

Fine, I thought. So I was quiet while we passed through the gate and into the back roads, making our way towards the access road that led to the highway and, eventually, the bridge back home. Quiet while he explained about the song and everything.

We weren't gonna make it to the bridge, though.

Rodney gripped the wheel and stared into the night.

"You want to know the truth?" he said.

I said I did and he took a breath and out it came.

The truth was Rodney had gone to ECCC about three weeks after the Governor had disappeared for the last time. He'd told me he was going shooting or whatever, and he'd driven into Pensacola to the campus. And he hadn't gone to meet with Troy.

There were only two ways in or out: the main entrance, with its guardhouses and striped gate arms and bollard-flanked card reader just past the WELCOME sign, and the west entrance, across from the Whataburger, where local students who lived at home could pass through a similar setup of card reader and gate arm and pair of guardhouses. Between these was a footpath for students who lived on campus to enter and exit at the apportioned times and with the written permission of the Office of Student Conduct. Every night, when Late Chapel was done, the gates of both entrances, mechanical extensions of the eight-foot-high iron fence that wrapped almost all of campus, would swing into place and lock tight.

Rodney had stood at the window of the gatehouse at the west entrance to Emerald Coast Christian College, waiting for the guard to finish scrolling through his tablet. Behind him had formed a line of boys with button-up shirts tucked into their belted khakis and girls in long skirts of pleated denim. They all had their phones out but weren't reading them; the screens all showed a square of code, which they had to scan to be let back in. Rodney was a buzz-cut golem in this line of children. The guard set his tablet down and looked up at him.

"You want the administration building. Tate Hall, seventh floor. Go down here past the sports center and hook a right. It's a big glass building shaped like a wedge."

"Like the golf club?"

"Like what you hit with a maul."

The guard slid a visitor's pass under the window.

"You'll need to keep that on you at all times."

Rodney clipped the pass to the left pocket of his T-shirt and thanked the guard again and walked into the campus. He'd been hearing that Troy Yarbrough and his people wanted to see him. Been hearing it for months. But finally he'd been convinced, and it was Rachael Kingdom who'd done the convincing.

She'd called him on the phone and at the sound of her voice he'd gotten breathless and, he told me, hard.

"Gross, dude," I told him. But I didn't know the half of how gross.

In a life marked by the appearances of large and startling women, this was the one who deranged his blood, made his heart shriek.

He made his way through the campus on paths lined with neat piles of foliage shorn by the winds of last night's storm, an early October roarer that'd rolled eastward from the Louisiana coast and weighed everything down with rain. On his drive over from Gulf Breeze he'd seen the collapsed roofs of various businesses, the great indentations of sheet metal, nothing new. The sun was high and the clouds had a singed look about them, smoke from somewhere or the beginnings of another storm. On the paths, college kids in sweat-drenched dress clothes eyed him strangely as he passed.

At the administration building another guard had to buzz him in. A shining door eight feet high swung open on pneumatics, and Rodney stepped inside.

"Just a second while I confirm your appointment," the guard said, easing back down behind his desk, a granite semicircle on which rested a metal-detector wand, a radio handset, and a tablet.

The guard called someone on the phone, said Rodney's name and "Yes, that's right." Then he got up and came around his desk and went to the elevators and held his badge in front of a card reader mounted to the wall. The doors of the elevator to the far left opened, and the guard reached a hand in to hold them so that Rodney could go in.

On the seventh floor a new receptionist bade him wait in an anteroom area of low leather chairs surrounded by wall-sized portraits of the Tates and ECCC alumni engaged in various acts of service or fellowship or charity. A younger Troy Yarbrough addressing a table of wide-eyed matronly girls. The receptionist's desk dominated a patch of wall on either side of which were two doors. The nameplate on the door on the left-hand side said Office of the University President and, below that, Rachael K. Yarbrough. The door on the right had no title, as if the name on the plaque, Troy Yarbrough, was all that needed to be said.

For over five minutes the receptionist didn't touch her phone, or her desktop, or the tablet propped up on its case. Rodney timed her by his watch. He couldn't see what she was looking at, and neither could he meet her eyes. When he finally took out his own phone and unlocked it and was about to begin to scroll, Troy Yarbrough's office door swung open and the receptionist told him he could go in.

He entered into a kind of foyer, a room before the room: on one side there was a polished buffet with a sword in a glass case and some documents arranged inside Lucite boxes, museum-style, with little notes of provenance—relics of the West Florida rebellions, he'd later learn, purchased by the Yarbroughs from old families in St. Francisville in Louisiana—and on the other side, a stuffed and mounted red wolf, posed in a moonward howl. Rodney couldn't make out the name on the brass plate. Light poured in from deeper in the office, and he had to blink a few times before he was sure who he saw walking out of it towards him.

"You can shut the door behind you," said Rachael Kingdom Yarbrough.

She wore a deep-blue skirted business suit cut like the uniform of a commander of a future army—high braided collar and cuffs. No jewelry, save the rings on her left hand.

Rodney shut the door and Rachael Yarbrough waved him to a pair of chairs set before an enormous oaken desk. He thanked her and chose one and sat with his ball cap in his lap while she turned and went over to the desk and grabbed the lip of it and turned herself to face him. He saw her repeated in framed desk-side portraits, reflected in the marble eyes of the heads of the animals mounted to the surrounding walls.

"I'm not trying to be that guy," Rodney said, "but is your husband coming?"

"He's away right now," she said. "But I thought we might be able to get started."

For a moment neither spoke, and Rodney took the opportunity to look around the room. There was a door in the adjoining wall and he imagined it led to Rachael Yarbrough's office and he wondered what it was like in there, and what he was doing in here with her.

He hadn't seen her since he was little. In the intervening years, she'd long been associated with both the Escambia County and Santa Rosa County Sheriff's Departments through her work with victims of human trafficking who often ended up in the Emerald Coast Youth & Women's Centers. She didn't do it much anymore, but the story went that whenever the department would get a good sting, some victim of human trafficking sitting double-crossed in a hotel room full of cops, Rachael Yarbrough herself would appear to offer the unlucky girl a choice: either come to the Center and get yourself right with the Lord, or go to jail. Most went with her, though what happened to them there was anyone's guess. There were jailhouse rumors from the ones who failed out or fled, of strange equipment, pregnancies, whole wings of big-bellied girls never seen again. But who was going to believe the loudest tweaker in the pod?

"Miss Rachael," Rodney said finally. "It's been a while."

She studied him for a moment. Then she pushed herself off the desk and went around it and sank into the high-backed kidskin chair.

"It doesn't feel that long to me," Rachael Yarbrough said. "I never stopped checking up on you. Did a little stalking. You were in law enforcement?"

"I tried, but I just wasn't cut out for it."

She nodded. "I hope you're comfortable with me bringing this up, but I never got to tell you properly how sorry I am for what happened to your family. I know Troy's dad helped after . . ."

Rodney's voice was like dirt on his tongue. "You did, though. You told me at the funeral."

She hadn't remembered that. But he had. He remembered everything with her. Rachael Yarbrough leaned forward in her chair, reached out with her voice. "I'm so sorry," she said. "You were so young."

"Yeah, well, that's why I tried the cop thing. I wanted to make sure people didn't get hurt like we did, but that's not what the job was."

"Then you started with DU3L. Is the prize money good? Sponsorships?"

Rodney shook his head.

"No permanent employment?"

"I don't know," he said. "Guess I haven't found somewhere I fit yet."

"What about with me?"

"Pardon?"

"With me. Do you think you'd fit with me?"

"Here?"

"You must be the kind of student who thinks the teacher lives at school," she said.

Rodney wasn't sure how to answer so he didn't. Rachael Yarbrough watched him and he saw a look in her eyes he knew down deep. He'd seen it when he was little but all that still felt like a kind of dream, even if it was stirring, awakening in him now.

"Troy's got his guards," Rachael Yarbrough said. "He's got his guys, and that's great. But they're his. They love *him*. They believe in *him*. And West Florida, of course. But in the end, where does that leave me?"

"You tell me."

"It leaves me vulnerable. In need of protection. In need of someone like you."

Rodney studied her. "You thinking violence?"

"I always am," she smiled.

"I'm just one person."

"You're a whole lot more than that," Rachael Kingdom said. "Remember, I have the gift of second sight, Rodney Woolsack. I see what's coming and, you know what, I see you there with me when it happens. I saw it when you were little. You do remember, don't you?"

"You don't forget your babysitter," he said. "I mean, some stuff's real clear, like the time you got cut off by Airport Boulevard and we were going to my house and you cussed a lot at the driver, screamed, and you told me not to say anything about that." He paused for a moment, tried to change the subject. He hooked a thumb back towards the taxidermied wolf.

"What happened to that one?" he said.

"Gracie? She was one of the first. A founding mother. We brought her up from Mexico along with seven others. She mated, had a litter, seemed like a real alpha. Then one night another female, younger, stronger, challenged her and tore out her throat, took Gracie's pups as her own. This was just after we'd moved them to the bigger enclosure and Gracie crawled and dragged a trail of blood that measured over a mile, still trying to fight."

Rodney looked over at the wolf

When he turned back to Rachael Kingdom she was close enough that he could see the ripples in the skin of her knees. The sun lines there. She swept her blazer back and stood with her hands on her hips, the slope of her belly standing out against the fabric of her skirt. He was breathing heavy and she knew it.

"You think Troy would try to . . . remove you?" Rodney said.

"Troy or someone else."

Rodney sucked his teeth. "Can I ask you something weird?"

"Shoot, gunfighter."

"Is there . . . something wrong with Troy? Some reason why now?"

She took a hissing breath. "What's wrong with Troy is that his brain is being eaten alive from the inside."

"Shut the fuck up."

"Excuse you," she said. "It's called a prion disease. Do you remember mad cow? You're not old enough to remember mad cow."

"You're kidding."

"Not one bit."

Rodney held his head in his hands and spoke to the floor. "Does he know how long he's got?"

"Troy doesn't know," Rachael Yarbrough said. "Or he did know and now he doesn't. Or there's some part of him that knew but now it's just a spongy patch of tissue in his skull."

He gaped at her. "That's crazy."

"Since when has something being crazy meant it isn't true?"

"Is—is he gonna die?"

"Oh, my, yes," she said. "Horribly."

Rodney looked up, fingers caging his face, imagining a worm-eaten log.

"West Florida's bigger than a person," she went on. "We've got the votes. I know we do. We've canvassed like crazy, and every poll, every shred of data backs it up. And *when* Troy dies, I'll be appointed to his seat, and when I'm appointed to his seat I will see to it that his legacy lives on and the bill passes in

D.C., and when that happens, I'm going to be the first governor of this state. And what I'm going to need, Rodney Woolsack, is a qualified candidate to serve as, say, First Gentleman. That's the why and the how."

"You want me?"

"Yes I do," she said. "Though I will admit you'd look good in a West Florida state trooper's uniform."

"What color y'all thinking?"

"Gray and gold. Maybe white."

"How'd Troy get this thing?"

"The doctors think he must've picked it up from a deer, eaten some infected meat. There's a whole strain of it going around in deer, been there for years, but it's only now showing up."

"The fuck."

"I never liked any of that hunting. Do you?"

"Hunt? Not even birds."

"That's wonderful," she said, and she went on talking about wonderful things, and as she spoke, Rachael Yarbrough took her hands off her waist and slid them down the sides of her skirt and hitched the hem up to her hips. Tight dark curls of pubic hair showed through sheer Spanx and spread beneath her belly in a triangle that ran almost from hip to hip.

"But there's something that worries me," she said.

"What?" She was looking at his face but he wasn't looking at hers.

"I asked if you remembered. When you were little."

"I think I do. Sometimes I feel like it was a dream. Like, I remember dreaming about that."

"About what."

"About what you did."

"What did I do?" she said. "Tell me."

Rodney shook his head. "You say it."

Rachael Kingdom stepped forward until the slope of her belly was right up to his nose and spoke to him low and slow.

"Fine," she said. "You want me to talk about how I went into your room and got in bed with you. How I tugged off your underwear and swung your knees over my shoulders. How I put my great, big mouth on you. Want me to tell you how you shuddered? How you shook like a foal? Your bony knees up against my temples."

"Jesus."

"I'd never done anything like that before. You were the first."

"I don't believe you."

"But do you believe *in* me?"

"Yes," he said.

"When you finished, I thought I'd killed you."

She had one hand in his hair and the other hooking open the crotch of her shapewear, and his face shook when he went for her.

Rachael Yarbrough let out a rasping breath, and then for a while he didn't hear anything but his throbbing blood and the sounds in her stomach. His eyes were shut and she was still talking.

"You believe in me," she said, although he didn't hear. "Yes, you do believe."

I wanted to say, Holy shit. I wanted to say, What the fuck. I wanted to say a whole lot of things when Rodney finished talking. But what I said was, "Sorry, man."

"Sorry?" he said. "The fuck you sorry about? Me eating pussy?"

"No, it's like—I'm sorry . . ."

"You sorry about what?" he said. Rodney looked at me. His face turned from the road and the SUV that'd pulled out ahead of us.

"I mean," I said, gathering my words, "about you being a kid and her doing that."

He was quiet for a second, glaring at me, and the brake lights of the SUV ahead came on. I flinched, but Rodney saw them in the corner of his eye and slowed without ever looking full-on back to the road.

"So, if it happened to you, you'd do what? No, tell me. This girl you have a crush on. She comes and gets with you and you can't even control it. You're just like, Oh my god I have had exactly this dream and gone to sleep each night thinking of something like this. You'd do what, exactly? Hate it? Fight?"

"I thought . . ."

"You thought what, fucker? You thought about how lucky you are to be here? You thought about how much you appreciate everything I do?"

The SUV braked again and we were slowing now.

I kept my head down. "I don't know," I said.

Rodney was still looking at me like I was the crazy one, only now we both had to squint because the windshield and mirrors filled with headlights that came flooding in behind us, and he suddenly snapped ahead and we lurched forward as he slammed the brakes, but it was too late. The car on our tail nosed up on our driver's-side flank like a shark and swung and pitted us, and Rodney swore and we were drifting, spinning out. He was whipping the wheel and telling me to take the fucking gun out of the glove box and the air flashed white.

We landed on the shoulder of the road with the tail of the truck half in a ditch. Rodney hit the gas but the wheels just spun and spun. Useless. I was hanging in my seat belt, bashed against my door, and when I sat up and peeked out the passenger-side window I saw we'd come to rest in such a way that our attackers faced us with their headlights and their vicious grilles in the north and southbound lanes. The only way out was over the ditch, through the woods.

But you know Rodney: he had to make a stand.

The doors of both cars opened and Rodney yanked me down. The windshield spidered and rounds went whomping against the chassis. I thought of the trucks I'd see when I was little, the ones that'd have those fake bullet-hole decals on the bumper. I always wondered why anyone would want that. You wonder about weird shit like that when someone's trying to kill you.

They kept firing and Rodney mashed me down into the seat and hauled me by the belt over the console and into the back seat. While I huddled with my hands over my head and the shots kept coming, Rodney was gearing up, pulling pieces he had stashed down in the undercarriage of the seat and elsewhere on his person. The volley went on and he crawled to the driver's-side door and swung it open and used the panel like a shield, firing from the edge of the door at the car in the northbound lane and then a handful of rounds over the hood at the car in the southbound lane.

Shouts, orders, and two guys rushed us from the northbound car.

I know he must've caught a few more because I heard them holler and I saw them lying there in the road later. He was glorious with a gun in his hand, that Rodney, but he'd gone through most of a magazine back there with Troy and the Electrician, and there came a point when he pulled and nothing came. I hated to see the way he looked then, astonished, a look arcing back towards the child he'd been on a night like this, when the world first came down on him.

I wondered, too, if the Electrician was out there, or even Troy Yarbrough. But I didn't hear their voices, or I couldn't tell. Anyway, it was loud as hell.

Rodney was saying, Fuck, and he was saying he was sorry, to me, I guess. I had my phone in my hand. It'd been in my pocket for the crash.

The rounds whomped off Rodney's door. He didn't move except to look at me. In four bursts he emptied one pistol and then another.

I was texting Leona. Because that's what you do when you're about to die in this country. You tell the ones who love you that you love them too.

Another volley of gunfire and then a stretch of silence long enough for the bugs in the wiregrass to start singing.

Oh baby, Leona said.

We sat there, bathed in the headlights of our enemies, who shouted now among themselves to come on. To get our asses. Rodney slumped back against the running board of the door and looked at me like, I'm sorry, I'm so sorry, but they were still coming, and another volley sounded and the front windshield bowed inwards and sagged in a million crinkled shards held together by their lamination. I was holding my phone like it could help me. A round caught Rodney in the neck and he threw himself back behind the door, gasping, clutching his throat, and I felt my crotch get cold. I squeezed my phone so hard my thumbs made those rainbows on the screen.

More gunfire and Rodney let go of his throat, held his hand in front of his face, and when he saw there was no blood his chin kind of fell and he was studying his shirtfront as the gunfire went on. There wasn't any blood there either but you could hear something broken up in his ribcage when he tried to breathe. In his lap and on the pavement of the road lay inch-wide riot slugs and scatterings of smaller rubber pellets. I saw it dawn on him that they wanted us alive, which was worse than dying.

The phone shook in my hands.

Oh fuck, Leona said.

"Hey," Rodney croaked at me. He said something else but I didn't understand at first. The guys shooting at us were hollering again and you could tell there were more of them in the car in the southbound lane. The one nearest to us had maybe one guy still armed and on his feet; he was the one shucking shells and laying on us with alternating bursts of ball shot and buck rubber.

When I looked over the console at Rodney again, there was blood this time. His right eye was spattered and swelling. The gunfire ceased and they were shouting about throwing something.

"Hey," Rodney said. "When I get up. Open your door and run. OK?"

"OK," I said.

"Whatever happens. Run for the woods."

I didn't say goodbye before I pocketed my phone and the flash-bangs came clanking over and he rose once more and emptied the very last of his guns at Troy's men even as everything went white and squealing. I didn't say anything—there wasn't any time or air and he wouldn't have heard me anyway, probably. The last I saw of Rodney, there on the roadside, was him in silhouette against the smoke and light, laying down enough cover for me to get out of the truck crawling, bullets whizzing, and then stumble through the ditch and up the embankment and into the trees. No chance to say, Hey, Dad, I love you, I'm sorry, you're insane but living with you has been the best part of my life, but I kept telling myself I said all that to him, and more. And that he turned to me then through the smoke and the muzzle flashes and the hail of rubber and lead and told me I'd done great, I was his, he loved me too.

I'm just gonna keep telling myself that's how it happened, until the day I die.

Maybe by then I'll be able to believe it.

CHAPTER SIX

BLOOD ON THE MOON, DUEL IN THE SUN

I ran like hell through the nightwoods, aimed myself in what I thought was the direction of State Road 281 and the bridge leading back to Gulf Breeze. My phone was pulsing in my pocket but I couldn't check it now. It was a miracle I'd held onto my phone at all, honestly, and it might sound silly but knowing that little heartbeat was Leona kept me going some.

The woods were broken at intervals by paths clear-cut for power lines and the rusted hulks of what had once been massive vehicles, bench-seated sedans bedecked in chrome, vehicles that had glided over the nightmare-perfect streets of the 1950s, back when everyone breathed lead.

In Spain's first occupation of West Florida, about five hundred years before, the land I ran through had been garrisoned for King Carlos I by the Yemassee people, a whole hell of a lot of whom, including the garrison commander and his whole family, were massacred in a single night by the Creeks, who felt they'd been repeatedly dicked over in trade. San Antonio de Punta Rasa. Blood on blood on blood in this country: scrape it off and there's just another layer waiting.

Of course, I'd thought wrong about the direction of the highway and the bridge. I didn't know the moon and stars as well back then, certainly not that awful early morning when everything seemed lost so I couldn't read my way by them, and anyway, if you're running and you glance up at the sky, you're liable to lose your footing, which I did. Shit on a fuck, I thought, which I remember clearly, because it's the stupidest thing you could be thinking at a time like this, when you might have to fight for your life at any moment.

Knocked flat and lying on my back, peering upwards through the gaps in the treetops, I couldn't find the moon at all, and the stars were just these smudgy streaks of light, like I was moving slow through hyperspace. The gunfire had ceased in the distance, and for a few moments I just lay there, trying to catch my breath. Ours here wasn't the only gunfire happening, of course, because the passage of the bill had cut the ribbon on the Florida Wars, full-scale, and there were battles raging all across the land, but you wouldn't know that where I was, on my back in the leaves. Sometimes, when it got good and quiet, I thought I could hear helicopters in the distance, jets, but you always heard jets and helicopters around here.

Now the new sound of four-stroke engines ripped like chainsaws through the woods, and I tried to sit up and see. Beams of light swept and shuttered across the tree trunks. I spat like I was tough, and the spit landed right back on my face so I had to wipe it off. Then I got back up and began to run again.

I felt lighter somehow now, like the fall had cleared me out. Maybe I was dead and my ghost was running and would haunt these woods forever and when, as Big Mike and surely Troy Yarbrough feared, there weren't any white people left in America, all of them having succumbed to despair or violence, my ghost would be running around these endless trees and whatever new inheritors lived among them would whisper and say, *Have you heard the story about the white boy in the woods?*

My breathing was easier too now. I'd always gotten stitches in my side as a little kid whenever I had to race at school, and Rodney hadn't been much for cardio during our summer training, but here I was, legs screaming, acid in my veins, Marathon Manning my ass off. But the branches and the briars and the roots were reaching for me, pulling me down again and again, and when I fell the earth was singing louder and louder each time. Why not just lie down right here and die?

The engines ripped and roared, circling, and I broke into a darker stretch of the woods, swallowed up in blackness, so I had to slow down and feel my way ahead. Everything I touched was alive in one way or another and that somehow made it worse, like I was going through a cave of rustling bugs or the mouth of a giant. Then the darkness burned away and I was swallowed in light.

They were four boys on a pair of armied-up Rangers mounted with spotlights, and they caught me there in the dark thicket like a fox. The drivers gunned their engines and I spun in the tangle of branches, trying to claw my way through.

They kept on gunning the engines, and I had my hands in front of me trying to block the blinding light and they were having fun, laughing, the drivers and the spotters, throwing all that noise and light at me.

I went to the ground and tried to crawl, tried to find a gap in the undergrowth that'd let me slip through. By then the drivers had dismounted and were coming for me and there wasn't anywhere to go, so I just looked pitiful, I guess. The spotters, standing in the rear racks, trained their beams on me and laughed, whooped instructions and encouragement.

I got into a crouch facing them and tried to coil up every atom of energy I had.

I tried to think of the Governor—not where she was right now, though I was pretty damn interested in knowing that, as well—but where she'd been back when I was a baby, what she'd done. I tried and I prayed there on the ground in the light, being laughed at and told exactly what was going to happen to me. Because of the spotlights blazing behind them, I couldn't see the drivers' faces, but I could see by their colonial uniforms they were the boys from the party earlier,

the ones who'd formed a rank. The honor guard or whatever. Or at least a detachment of them. The rest, I figured,
were either out patrolling elsewhere, or they were back at
the compound helping Troy Yarbrough do whatever he was
doing to Rodney.

One of the drivers got in front of me and I could hear
the other circling behind. The one in front wore chest armor
and was carrying a short machine gun. The plate carrier on
his chest had Troy's wolf stencil and a patch that said Muzzy
on it. He stood with his legs spread wide, framing my face.

"All right," Muzzy said. "Tie him."

I thought about Rodney, too, and a shrieky growl grew in
my throat and I couldn't help it—it just came out. Rumbling
and yet high-pitched, like something metal falling apart. I'd
heard a coyote make a noise like that once, when I was little.
It was the fall after the spinal tap. I just let myself out one
night while everybody was sleeping and walked down the
street and out of the subdivision onto the access road. The
air had gotten colder overnight and the ditches and the grass
were quiet and the road I walked down was empty. I could
see headlights skipping through the boards of fences maybe a
half mile down. The cool air seeped through the holes in my
Crocs and I felt tightness and a tingle take ahold of my back,
and I turned and there was the coyote. Hackles up. Muzzle
down at the blacktop, sniffing my footprints. Its mouth was
open and I could see its teeth, its tongue lolling, and then
the coyote raised its head and made that noise, the one I was

making on the floor of the forest. A blast from the horn of an F-150 nearby rumbled up in the next moment and sent both me and the coyote skittering, but for a second there it was just us and that sound. I think it had babies somewhere, something to protect. Or maybe it was trying to tell me something.

I don't know. But the coyote's howl was in my throat and I sprang at Muzzy, trying for a tackle. But his boot caught my forehead and then they were on me, knees in my back, driving me into the earth, which didn't want me at all now, it seemed. The hard-packed ground pressed up against me, like the earth was forcing me up and these guys were holding on for dear life. One took my hair in a tac-gloved fist and yanked my head back and I could see his face—young, soft-cheeked, smiling a mouthful of small round teeth. The strange sensation of someone about to go in for a kiss.

"Kick him, Muzz," said the one who had my hair, and the other strode around and gave me the boot again and I told myself, Don't cry, don't cry, don't cry.

If I was a liar I'd say I didn't, I'd say I kept it together, which was the second thing I told myself to do while they kicked me and punched me in the back of the head and the kidneys. The third thing was that I was gonna fucking kill them.

Now, I hadn't seen all that many people die thus far, and none of them super slowly, but that third thing is something damn near everybody says when you've got them pinned and they know what's coming and there's nothing they can do about it.

I guess it's more of a promise than anything. Or even a wish.

Unfortunately, this wish doesn't come true for about ninety-nine percent of the people who make it, just like it wouldn't come true for me that night. These fuckers wouldn't die by my hands.

Once the boys decided they were done beating on me, I was gagged and zip-tied at the wrists and ankles and Muzzy went behind with a Gerber and swung it open like a butterfly knife and clipped the ends of the zip ties so there wouldn't be anything for me to break off and use as a pick. I guessed the Electrician had trained them, and I was wondering how many people they'd done this to already—or if I was the first, the start of the next phase of Troy Yarbrough's state. Then they had me by the armpits and I was hauled upright and laid in the Ranger's rear basket rack.

Muzzy climbed into the driver's seat and slipped his machine gun into a case mounted midseat while his spotter slung his own gun across his chest and climbed the rack where I was lying, folded, fetal. He took the toe of his boot and rolled me so I was facing out, away from him and the driver. Then he planted one foot on my back and left it there. My shirt was bunched and the metal of the rack was cold on my skin. I imagined the spotter in a Captain Morgan pose, like some hunter with his kill.

"Hey, Muzz," said the driver of the other Ranger. "Can we head on back to the house while y'all take care of this?"

"Nah," Muzzy said, "we need you riding escort. There's a lot of wild shit tonight."

Then the driver was arguing with him and now the spotter of his car asked if it wasn't a good idea to maybe tie my bitch ass down, so I couldn't throw myself out while they were in motion, and then the other spotter was telling everybody to hold up while he got the winch straps out. I thought about hunting and I thought about Troy and I tried to tell myself that the man was dying, that he'd get his, that even if me and Rodney were dead that wouldn't change what was coming for that motherfucker.

I heard the other spotter leap down and unlatch a lid, and then the sound of him sifting through whatever was in there.

"Don't worry about that shit," Muzzy called to him. "Let's move."

"Just let me dick with it a second."

"We ain't got dickin' time. Just carry it."

"For real," the spotter who stood above me said, bringing his heel down on my ear and holding it there. "This little bitch isn't going anywhere anyway."

I bit the insides of my cheeks. Thought about human brains turned to sponge.

"Do y'all eat deer meat?" I said.

The sound of my voice surprised me. The way it can if you watch a video of yourself. Except on videos, if you're like me, you sound like a tinny distant shrunken version of yourself. This wasn't like that. I sounded like a corpse that's come out of its grave with dirt in its mouth and has got something to say.

"What?" said the one with the boot on my ear. "The fuck you say?"

"I said, do y'all eat deer meat?"

The one standing on me laughed and said, "You're about to eat shit, motherfucker. Or dick." The laughter spread to the other Ranger, along with suggestions of what I might be made to eat. Mostly it was dicks and orifices. "Maybe your boyfriend's," said one voice. "Maybe your own," said another.

But Muzzy didn't join them, or at least he didn't offer a menu item.

He was chewing on what I'd said.

"Yeah, I hunt," Muzzy said, growing serious on this subject. "Only ethical way to get your meat, you ask me."

"You ever eat deer meat with Troy?"

The spotter pressed his boot on me. "It's called venison, dumbfuck."

"Yeah, what's your point?" Muzzy said.

"You know why he looks like that?"

"Looks like what."

"Like a fucking skeleton," I said, and then I started laughing because I was thinking about Troy's brain Swiss-cheesed and then all of theirs and I wanted to explain but apparently I just found it too damn funny. Muzzy didn't, though.

He got down and came around to the rack and stood there studying me. He was holding his machine gun across his chest like it was a child he was trying to protect and I was some bum on the street corner, ranting.

"Hey," the driver of the other Ranger called to him. "You said we need to go, Muzz, so let's fucking go."

Muzzy didn't seem to hear him but closed the distance between us, jerked his chin at the spotter. "Sit him up," he said.

The spotter blew a breath like, If you say so, took his foot off my ear, grabbed another fistful of my hair, and yanked me upright.

"You're all gonna die," I said, spinning, about to topple if it weren't for the fist tugging my scalp. I swayed in his grip like a blind man, oracular, and said, "Your brains are gonna melt and run out your ears."

Muzzy hefted his gun and whipped the buttstock at me. Broke my nose. I wobbled there in the rack and when I shook my head to clear the blur there was blood all over my face and up in my nose and my throat.

"Do you know where you are?" Muzzy said.

"Yeah," I said.

He cracked me with the stock again. This time across the cheek.

"I didn't say speak, bitch."

"OK," I said.

The next blow broke my cheek and left me twisting there in the spotter's grip, my face and my shirt awash with blood.

"Well, now," Muzzy said, "I hate to tell you but you're in a world of hurt tonight." Muzzy squatted down so he could look me in the face. "Your boyfriend's back there with the Electrician, having a whole lot of fun. You saw his dog, right? Know what that dog likes to do? Well, lemme tell you: the Electrician's got himself a little thing of musk, like what a girl dog's pussy smells like. Me, I don't know what girl dog pussy smells like, but that dog smells it—he goes fuckin' nuts. He'd stick his dick in a hornets' nest if the Electrician dabbed that shit on it. And I guarantee you he's gonna dab it on your boy back there. His mouth. His asshole. I seen it. We came in with this One Florida gal, old bitch, and he had her in there and let me tell you." Muzzy made a long high sound of admiration, or maybe a howl. "That's that man's idea of fun. That's what he does to people who fuck around with us, much less than what he does to people who fuck the fucking boss's lady." He sort of winced, like he saw something in my eyes. Bent closer. "Don't get jealous. He might've started already but you won't miss out. We're gonna tote you over there so you can join in too."

I couldn't help the way my eyes must've looked—wet and full of fear and rage. But the rage was like a match thrown into a well, sinking in the dark.

"Now, looks to me like you got the point, deer meat. But just in case you think you're gonna pull some shit, like, on the way you decide to roll around, throw yourself, talk shit, talk anything, honestly, I'm gonna hit the brakes, go over to the

toolbox, and get me a pair of pliers and pull your motherfucking teeth out. Got it?"

I said nothing.

He held the gun up again. "Speak, bitch."

"Yeah," I said. My eye was about swollen shut and pain
was hammering from my cheek to the back of my skull. "Got
it."

"No, you don't," Muzzy said, standing up and readying to
walk back to the driver's seat. "What you got is a long way to
go, bitch. I haven't even gotten to the bad part yet."

After the shoot-out on the access road, they'd taken Rodney,
wounded, to an old deer slaughterhouse at the edge of the old
West Florida Estates, the neighborhood Pawpaw had managed
to get about half-built before the feds came down on him for
fraud. The one him and us and all who followed in the years
to come were supposed to oversee and lead from the mansion
house, where instead Troy Yarbrough's party had been. The
Estates occupied roughly twenty-something acres, cut out of
the slash pine, running to the north of the mansion property,
separated from it by a road lined with crepe myrtles. The
plan had been for forty housing lots, but only one street had
units built, chateau-style, like the ones I'd grown up in back
in Louisiana. Even thirty years later, most of them remained
unfinished, yellowed Tyvek paper flapping in the breeze, surrounded in acreage that looked for all intents and purposes

like muddy battlefields marked with ancient tread tracks and mounds of earth and sacks of concrete turned to brick and the snarled remains of trees uprooted during the first Bush administration.

When Rachael Kingdom's parents had bought it all with the help of Don Yarbrough, their plan was to use the mansion as a meeting place for ECCC events, and the neighborhood as housing for trainees from the college. Instead, during the first decade of Rachael and Troy's marriage, after Troy had hired the man now known as the Electrician to splatter Rachael's parents all over a luxury condominium in the foothills of the Kenscoff Mountains near Port-au-Prince, Rachael and Troy turned the land into a kind of hunting camp for men of influence.

In what had once been cane-cutting time, antlered deer fell by hand-drawn arrows, then by bolts and the fire of automatic rifles and, later in the hunting season, as if time curved backwards to make a circle, by muzzle-loaders. Hands accustomed to keyboards went clumsily about the motions of the distant past that all our tomorrows would grow to resemble, tipping powder from horn to muzzle, drawing the tamping rod up and down, while cell phones slept in waterproof plastic pouches in their pockets. These men used these trips and Troy himself as a means of shoring up support in the western edge of the county, to show how tough and real they were. Governors, the sons of future presidents, they all brought home their kills as meat from the on-site renderer, which Troy had ordered built in the house on the edge of the clear-cut land. Three more he'd had converted into shoot-houses, places to train his boys in various suburban warfare scenarios.

Troy must've had designs, even back then, on making some kind of army for himself. He's an American after all, and when we aren't content with one-man armies, we try to gather like-minded toadies unto ourselves. That's why, even now, when I see some politician or county sheriff looking like he went on a diet, see a certain twitch at the corner of his mouth like an invisible claw is pulling it aside, I'll know he probably went hunting with Troy.

Troy's men dragged Rodney into that house, which long ago had been planned as a living room, a place where a family would gather in the warmth of prime-time television, and instead had been stripped to the studs and set with a pair of tables for processing the kills—eight-foot slabs of bloodstained pine. Off in the corner another pair of tables, smaller, set with Mighty Bite #8 meat grinders. Just off-center in the room stood a weight-bearing column, something you'd hang pictures on, that your little brother would run smack into when you were playing inside like you weren't supposed to. There was a long plank fixed to it at a sixty-degree angle and Rodney was brought to it unconscious, bound there by the hands and feet.

I heard about the video later. They had cameras set up in all the rooms. Everywhere on the property. I couldn't watch it for long, but I'd see the room, see the dog where it was tied. See the old blood and the new. The motorcycle batteries and the cords. The water jug on its side. I've seen the wasting herds myself since then, too. Those mutant deer: they'll amble right on up to you, big-eyed wraiths dripping drool from their muzzles. Whenever I see them, I think of that room and Rodney.

He'd already suffered plenty in his life, but who can say when it's enough?

The Electrician came in with his dog on a lead and he handed it off to one of the boys who'd hauled Rodney in. The boy tied the leash to the leg of the far table, and the boy stood and the dog sat watching while the man went about his work.

It was true: the Electrician had a small black glass bottle secreted on his person, like the essential oils sold by someone's aunt. But he didn't bring that out first thing. I guess he wanted to show Rodney what he'd learned while serving our country. He told the boy to get his phone out and the boy did so and thumbed the screen until he found what the Electrician wanted. The boy hit play and sat the phone on the tabletop beside him and the song began to play.

You can't really tell what's playing during the video. Something with a lot of strings.

Classical shit. *Carmina Burana*. Nazi walkup music.

The boy folded his arms and the dog shifted on its haunches, panting.

Meanwhile, the Electrician went to what had once been planned for a kitchen and filled a plastic water jug he found there and came back with it, sloshing, in one hand. With the other he pulled a bandana from his back pocket and laid it across Rodney's face, Rodney looking like some old-time stage-coach robber as the Electrician cinched the knot and stood again, took up his jug, and poured.

A strawberry supermoon had risen that night. When we came out of the woods into the clear-cut acres, headed for the slaughterhouse, I could see everything racing away behind me. I bumped and rocked in the rack, my mind about as stripped and ruined as the land we passed through. Here and there lay evidence of use—a firing range, barrels and bales and the cutout shapes of men they'd pasted with the faces of their enemies. A firepit with a burn barrel at its heart, looking like a bomb had dropped.

Just like I'd be lying if I said I didn't cry that night, I'd be lying even worse if I told you I didn't pray. Not before or since have I given any time to what most folks here think of as God. The god of my ancestors, the absolute rip-off god of the Yarbroughs. But on that night I prayed and prayed and promised my soul.

And then we slowed. I felt a new fear, worse, something I'd thought was impossible. I wanted to vomit, rocking there in the rack, suddenly halted. But the spotter didn't get down. Nobody did. And there was a sense in the dark of something enormous moving and a voice went, "Whoa. Whoa." Then they were all saying, "Ma'am," asking whoever it was what she was doing out right now.

"None of your beeswax," Riley Rae said to them. "Can you believe that?" she said to someone else.

She was on a horse with a glowing bridle and tack, some kind of night-safety neon, which I discovered when she rode around to examine where I lay trussed. The heaving beast leaving tracers on the air. She was streaming the whole thing live, her phone rigged up in the tack. That's who she'd been talking to.

"What's he doing?" she asked, pointing at me like I was a frog in a jar. "He's all tied up in there." And to her followers: "I don't know who this kid is."

I tried to say my name, who I was, that she'd seen me earlier that night. Every time I tried to move my mouth the pain squeezed harder, like it'd pop out my eye.

"He's nothing," said Muzzy.

"Trespasser," said the spotter.

Riley Rae went, "Hmmmm." The horse made those flapping noises with its lips.

Meanwhile, I was still trying to force words out of my mouth, thinking maybe if I could get her to speak to me, to recognize me as another human being, they might, too, and this would all be over.

I said, "H-hey?"

She said, "Are you talking? He's talking right now." She folded over the reins in her hands and bent down, craning at me. "What do you want?"

"Help?" I managed.

"Oh," she said, disappointed. She straightened herself in the saddle, said, "I'm sorry, really. But my mom and dad are fighting and . . . you know how it goes." She spoke to her followers, saying, "Right. Right. Love you."

I shut my eyes. Tears and blood and snot all down my face again. My head felt like it was going to burst. Riley was still talking, hadn't stopped the whole time.

Then I saw headlights.

Two sets of them, burning across the ruined ground. They were mounted on a four-wheeler and I saw in the moonlight the bright red armor fender flares as it neared. Maybe that's the face of god after all, when you get down to it, because the god I want to believe in is a woman raring up in the saddle of a furious machine, one fist gripping the handlebars and the other squeezing off rounds.

It was Leona on her Bonaparte. The greatest thing I've ever seen. Racing over the field, spraying fire. My god and my love and my West Florida, too.

She'd ridden out of Gulf Breeze and straight into the myths and legends of our land that night, blaring "Let the Sunshine In" over her handlebar speaker in a loop in tribute to her grandmother, who made her promise before she left that she'd come back. People who were there, caught in the snarl of traffic that started when people fled the areas where the open fighting had begun, still talk about the sight of her streaking over the rise of the bridge in the shoulder of the northbound lane, with that song going, an image captured on dashcams and phones shot out windows and held in trembling hands.

"The fuck—?" said the spotter above me, before the gunshots cut him off. A hail of rapid fire tore across his chest and sprayed the other Ranger and its occupants and sent Riley Rae's horse shrieking. I saw that beast and its rider canter wild past me and a hunk of meat come off the horse's flank, Riley Rae ducking close to the horse's neck and urging it on into a charge. I lost sight of her when Muzzy hit the gas. His spotter fell over me, squalling, gutshot, and I wriggled him off and watched him spill out as we raced away.

That Ranger didn't have the speed of little Bonaparte, though, and I think Muzzy was hit because we kept jerking back and forth, like he couldn't keep the wheel straight. I saw her headlights grow and grow, my heart in my throat, and she passed us and slashed into our path and the next thing I knew I was thrown out of the rack and rolled along the dirt maybe fifty yards until I skidded to a stop.

I heard boots scrabbling and random gunfire and then Muzzy screeching, cussing, saying, No, no, no, like he couldn't believe it, until Leona went over and destroyed his face with three rounds point-blank.

I rolled over in the wheel ruts, pushed myself up on my elbows and started crawling over to where Bonaparte stood, and I pulled myself behind him as more gunfire started up from the direction of the Estates and beams of laser sights whipped our way. Troy's boys. A lot of them.

Those on foot advanced, raking ahead with two-round bursts of gunfire. Clouds of dust kicked up all around. Leona hunched over her rifle and hustled over, threw herself down on the ground beside me. Another sound began to fill the air, and above that, a droning whine. She set her rifle down and took me by the armpits and lifted me up, pulled me close as the shots pinged off poor Bonaparte, and she crawled us backwards over the bullet-riddled ground until we slipped over a hard-packed lip of mud and slid down into the swale.

"I'm here," she said, pressing my face to where her chest would be if she hadn't been wearing body armor, pressed me so that my busted cartilage squeaked in my head and hurt even worse than before. I tried to wriggle loose, and she must've thought I thought she was somebody else so she kept saying, "It's me. It's me. It's me," and squeezed harder as the bullets tore Bonaparte to shreds. The plating crunched a couple times and I imagined the gas tank going up, movie-style, in a column of fire.

Leona held me tight. I knew she was strong before, but this was like no other strength I'd ever felt. Flip a car off your kid strength.

Except in this case, you were getting fired on while you lifted the car, and the bullets were zinging off the chassis and all around the ground. Finally I just gave up and let her do it. While Leona squeezed and rocked me, the gunfire kept on and a flock of clouds passed over the pale red moon and threw the land around us into shadow. Across the field, our attackers closed in, shouting orders back and forth. Firework volleys. Hissing tires.

Leona held me and I said to myself if I'd known six months ago this would be the way I'd die, squeezed to death by awesome love, I'd have been cool with it.

The boys advancing on us were maybe a hundred yards away by the sound of their voices and the concentration of their fire. Bonaparte would never ride again but he did his job that night, took every round of theirs like a champ. But I knew he wouldn't hold out as a shield forever, and the other Rangers were just about shredded too. The boys were close enough I could tell their voices apart.

Leona held me at wrist's length and nodded the way she'd come.

"Look," she said, and I saw them, fanning out across the darkened field, a dozen orbs of ruby light hovering waist-high in the air like fireflies.

"The fuck," I said, and Troy's boys were saying the same. They called out to put eyes on this shit. Shouted for confirmation. Called out to know what it was.

I thought maybe it was the cops or the army, a strike team in ghillie suits, come to put a stop to this, that sanity would arrive like a parent picking you up at the end of the day. But the lights were weirdly low, about eye level. Then one of the orbs went *vreem*, and the sound was carried across the field.

The orbs pulsed, changing colors. Then the air beat down on us, whipped by wings and rotors, and suddenly the night sky was full of burning metal.

I gasped and we both turned in each other's arms to look skyward.

High above, across the fading face of the moon, flares issued from the flanks of gunships and fell in arcs of smoke and light that drifted over the wide field of mud and broken trees and cast everything in a yellowish light: her, me, and up above, old Bonaparte and the dead boys and their rides. Further off, in the direction Leona had come from, about a half dozen gundog quads with rifles mounted to their backs were advancing over the open ground.

"Jesus Christ," I said. "It's the Governor."

"Are those hers?" Leona gawked. "Goddamn. You weren't lying," she said, without waiting.

Before I could tell her I would never lie to her, the quads opened up with their guns. The drill-buzz of rapid fire repeated again and again as the quads moved forward in that bouncing gait, firing as they went. Leona helped me to my feet and we climbed up out of the swale to where Bonaparte stood shredded and smoking, and we leaned there together, watching.

The quads were far ahead, almost to the road that ran parallel to the Estates, and I saw others work along the margins of the woods, mopping up whoever had tried to run there. Above us, in the vaults of clouds, flocks of smaller drones peeled off and swept down over the rooftops of the Estates, the larger aircraft heading on in battle-spread formation for the big house, party lights still blazing.

We limped our way in the wake of the quads, passing through the dying and the dead, Leona giving the groaners and the ones who dragged themselves like fallen squirrels on their bellies an extra round or two, because she was taking no prisoners.

"Save it," I said, looking at her belt and gesturing with my mashed hand toward the roofs of the houses rising now out of the flare light and the smoke. "You don't know what they got up there."

She grinned. "I know what's coming for them, though," and we both thought of the Governor.

Further on, she stopped by a skinny boy with freckled cheeks and a bowl cut lying there in his sock feet, gaping wide-eyed at nothing. She eased me down so I could grab the sidearm he wore at his waist. I clipped the ugly little Sig to my waistband and we kept going.

To the east the woods were glowing, like some gigantic craft had landed there. Its thrusters lit the underbrush on fire. I was so spellbound, my feet caught and I tripped. Leona shouldered me up, but I couldn't take my eyes off the sight as the glow grew and swelled into a dome of light that turned the sky the color of Leona's batting helmet.

I heard a man's voice raised in panic behind us, turned and saw one of Troy's men who must've hidden in the western woods burst from the trees and come stumbling into the field, where he twisted, jerked, and fell flushed. As he lay there a handful of small drones whirled down and lit above him, gyring like crows.

When we stepped down out of the muddy field onto the pavement of the road, the flames were roaring out of the busted windows all along the single avenue of the West Florida Estates. Nothing but bodies and blackened siding, shreds of Tyvek carried by the updraft and sent whirling like dust devils across our path. Now I feel like a fool that we went straight down that street that night without fear of sniper fire, but I also think we knew that nothing else could touch us. We were perfect and unstoppable, or at least that's how I felt, until the dawn broke full and we made it to the mansion, where the duel was about to take place.

The Governor told me later that when she saw Rodney step out of the burning slaughterhouse, she cried for the first time in years. He strode straight out to her, where she stood in what would've been a street, in the heart of the shell of the Estates, and embraced her. The present is a scorpion and history's its tail, bent to sting itself, she said, and here they were again. Rodney came down the steps of the front porch, smoke gathering in the windows behind him. He'd left the Electrician back inside, lashed to the post with his dog, the flames closing in. I don't know how he got his hands free—the video doesn't show and I never got the chance to ask—but he did, and when the Electrician came to douse him with the jug again he'd grabbed the man's wrist and wrenched him down and locked on his throat with his teeth. Rodney's face was smeared with blood and he let go of Destiny a little and they stood back from each other at arm's length. By nightfall, when the Estates and the mansion and houses across the state were still smoldering, Destiny would be ready to set out and go among the people with her cards and her currency. She knew that what people want most when they are hurt or in pain, the thing they ask in their moments of greatest fear and outrage, is for someone, something to come and make it stop.

She said the first thing he asked for was me.

I believe her, because it wasn't long before me and Leona had come upon the pair of them ourselves. We'd made it through the burning neighborhood and back to the mansion, the remains of the party strewn around the lawn, toppled wicker on the pool deck, scattered folding chairs draped with well-dressed corpses.

The congressman stood half-naked on the pool deck, armed with pistols strapped across his chest and a long gun ready to leap to his shoulder. He was wobbling as if he'd been shot, or maybe it was the disease eating him at last to the bone. Above him, on the portico, Rachael Kingdom waited, watching Rodney and Destiny.

Troy staggered forward, waved his weapon and called out to Rodney.

"You trashy piece of shit," he said. "You fucking nothing. I've been owing you this your whole pathetic life. My family supported you. We bought this property when your dad didn't have a dime. You, your family, your whore of a mother, you all leeched off of us, off my dad, and this is how you repay it? Now you made a whore out of my wife, and tonight, now, when everything is . . . here . . . now . . ." He shook, sobbed a second, hugged his rifle, and then he looked up. "I swear to God in heaven you're not leaving here alive."

"Well," Rodney said. "I won't be the only one."

Troy screamed in rage and Rodney, meanwhile, stalked along the other side of the pool with his hitching stride, in his hand a pistol that Destiny had given him not long after he stepped out of the burning house.

It was Pawpaw's Colt .38 Special. I only know that because later it became part of the record. But at the time, all I knew was that he had it in his right hand and his elbow was slowly swinging out. He set his feet and eased into his stance while Troy went on ranting, raising his rifle. I wanted to call out to him. I wanted to go and take his hand, but with one eye on Rachael Kingdom, the Governor shook her head at me, mouthing, *Go*.

Leona took my hand and we backed away, toward the row of camellias that grew along the edges of the pool deck, trash blown all up in their branches. On the other side was the boathouse and the docks. Leona said, "Come on," and pulled my hand and tried to duck under the boughs, but I turned back when I heard Troy Yarbrough fire, two quick bursts.

A white tablecloth had blown and snagged in the branches and the saw-toothed leaves like a flag in the wind, as Rodney, shot through but still on his feet, raised the Colt and blasted a hole through the lower portions of Troy Yarbrough's face.

"Come on," Leona said. But I couldn't.

Yarbrough stayed on his feet, yowling and trying to swing his rifle up again, until Rodney shot him again and Troy Yarbrough's head fell to the side and dangled like a hangnail off his shoulder.

Rodney went a few steps, staggered, and came to rest against a bar cart. I cried out Rodney's name and the Governor's, but she didn't seem to hear me. She was walking over to him, her own sidearm drawn and held out, sweeping the way clear as she went to kneel at Rodney's side. Leona tried to pull me away but I tore free of her and ran to where the Governor was bent over him, taking his face in her golden hand.

He was already dead when I got there.

I wouldn't see Rachael Kingdom flee or know how she made her escape until much later, when all of this was news and posts and footage. In the famous images, taken after his death, Rodney is folded upon himself, his hand shaped to hold the ghost of a gun. From his body was recovered a quantity of lead weighing no less than a pound.

My eyes were shut and burning, and when I opened them the Governor was squeezing my hands in hers, trying to press something there for me to take.

It was the rodeo ring. Rodney had given it to her, told her he wanted me to have it. I wear it now, with tape wadded in the band to keep it fast until the day it fits. The Governor carries the Colt. I can't say where the bullets went, the ones they took out of Rodney. Maybe they were secreted away and someday they'll be passed around as keepsakes, artifacts of the Florida Wars.

But something has to be over for there to be artifacts and museums to house them, and this is far from over yet.

The Governor squeezed my hands, her eyes brightening as she looked behind me.

"Come on," Leona said, her hand on my shoulder.

The Governor had risen now and was striding toward the house and I let myself run, rush toward the water with Leona. We were working along the hedges when the leaves around us were torn away by gunfire. Across the pool, coming for us with some kind of machine pistol in one hand and cradling in the other an orb of milky stone, was none other than Riley Rae.

"You bitch!" she called, and squeezed the trigger again. "You killed my horse, you trash-ass bitch!"

Riley Rae fired again and we hit the ground and started crawling for the boathouse, tufts of sod kicking up all around, but soon all I heard was Riley Rae cussing. I looked back and saw her heft the rifle high and shake it, her teeth bared and an animal noise. The thing had jammed, or else we'd have been dead.

Before I could blink, the barrel of Leona's rifle appeared over my shoulder and she sent Riley Rae screaming to the ground. Leona slung her rifle back across her shoulder and took my hand again, and we ran across the lawn to the boathouse as the air filled with sirens and the lights of police cars and armored vehicles swarming down the gravel drive.

A green Santa Rosa sheriff's cruiser ripped around the side of the house, sending furniture and catering carts flying as it skidded in and braked. We'd made it to the boathouse when the cruiser came to a halt.

There were speedboats and fishing boats in dry dock, winched up by straps and hanging over our heads. I looked back at the big house, saw the cruiser's door fly open and Claudia Laval step out with her service weapon drawn.

I don't know if she saw me. We haven't spoken since. Our worlds have grown distant, and mine has no time for the law.

"There," Leona said, and pointed to a floating dock where a pair of Jet Skis sat on rollers. She asked if I could drive one of these things and I said no, and we hopped down onto the floating dock, shoes slipping on the wet plastic links. Leona went to the nose of the nearest Jet Ski and unhooked its tether from the dock, grabbed the handlebars, and walked it down to the water. She swung herself into the seat, cranked the engine, and slapped the vinyl behind her for me.

Out on the bay, the wind was blowing at us from the southwest and it gathered up the racing tide, pushed these great big swells our way, and we rode the waves from trough to peak like ramps, so that for much of our escape we skipped in the direction of Butcherpen Cove like a stone. I kept my hands around Leona's waist. I suspect I'll never be so free again as in those moments when we crested and the spray burst all around us and we were airborne, throttling from one wave to the next, with the dawn full and awesome on the water and the smoke rising from the distant shores of home.

GO WEST

The Florida Wars went on all summer long. Between the First Battle of Garcon Point in June and the heart of hurricane season in late August, when the storms slammed in like great big bad mamas home from work and howling for us all to quit it, the fighting spread across the coast, as neighbors struck out at perceived opponents, known enemies, each other.

Before nightfall of the first day of fighting, without any witnesses to say otherwise, the blame for the death of Troy Yarbrough had been laid at the feet of the beleaguered One Florida org, whose spokespeople were either killed or hiding in the safety of the interior. Unsatisfied, momentarily rudderless, and murderously confused, the Yarbroughs' so-called Army of West Florida fought everywhere and anyone they could, while the bill sat in Tallahassee on the desk of the fake-ass governor there, who now insisted he would under no circumstances put pen to paper until both sides came to their senses and called a truce. The televised pleas and official proclamations to this effect were readily accepted by the One Florida folks, ignored completely by the Yarbrough forces, led now by Rachael Kingdom, who addressed them before billowing red wolf flags while a bandaged Riley Rae sang their anthem. By the end of the first week of hostilities, there were reports of firefights breaking out as far west as Dauphin Island in Mobile Bay and as far east as Lake City. Because theirs was far from the only side, now that was becoming increasingly clear, as people flocked to ours and the osprey rose on flags and shirts, spray-painted diving across the sides of cars turned battlewagons.

I wouldn't see the Governor again for months, but she was everywhere.

She appeared to the people in commercials between the videos they watched and in banner ads that moved with their scrolling and in persistent boxes with multiple Xs you could never click away from. In optimized search engine results and in promoted posts across various social media platforms and in their own posts and those they shared and in paywalled long-form investigative articles, which pored over the murky details of her past. She appeared on digital billboards from Tampa to Mobile. Her face smiling down on the commuters and truckers and vacationers and those making long trips moving weight. Increasingly, the image displayed was only her metal arm flexed before the words GO WEST.

Decommissioned fortresses overlooking the passes and the bays were taken by surprise, subversion, direct assault, park rangers frog-marched through the entrance gates and past the little boxes where you paid your fee. Weedy, overgrown battlements were stalked once more by armed men, who cleared sand from gunports through which soldiers in woolen uniforms had once watched ironclads and gunboats steam. At night, fires burned in the hearts of the former barracks and the defenders told stories to pass the time. In daylight, from gunless casemates, they searched the skies for helicopters or swarms of drones and the water for ships and what flags they flew.

The first naval battles off these shores in almost two centuries went down between speedboats and other pleasure craft with ensigns of the red wolf or the osprey whipping from their sterns, college banners flown subordinate—snarling tigers and toothy gators and bulldogs and the whitewashed decapitated head of Osceola. Only occasionally seen was the flag of the nation, which got ever smaller in the rearview of our speeding lives, same as its guardsmen—those who bothered to report—and the fighter jets and other combat aircraft grounded on the bases.

During the July Fourth Weekend Ceasefire, the Governor appeared in disguise and went among the people unnoticed until days later, when someone pointed her out in photos posted online. In the cities, dirt-bike squadrons patrolled the edges of neighborhoods into which Black people had once upon a time been forced, now bounded by walls against which fresh waves of white madness hurled themselves and broke. Throughout the countryside, electrical power substations were bombed and cell phone towers sabotaged, so that the tail end of summer grew long and hot as hell.

We laid up, Leona and me, in safe houses and abandoned stores, sticky and still like bugs in the throat of a pitcher plant. She read me crumbling paperbacks that told of futures like our own, my head in her lap, my mind swimming.

The Governor appeared in dreams, where she assumed the role of accessory to crimes or was the object thereof. She appeared to some as an object of desire, in fantasies and in the bodies of significant others in bed, so that a generation of children could be said to have been gotten by her spectral influence. She appeared in conspiracies which saw her leading a great internal resistance to the decadence of the American government, or in the control of secret societies masking as the same, or under the malign influence of an alien race. In cartoons published in newspapers' digital editions and in pornography, deepfaked or animated or crudely impersonated. She appeared to our enemies as an object of desire and envy, but most of all dread. She appeared in games sculpted out of digital blocks, or as the skins of the characters they played. She appeared in prayers: for her deliverance, for her supremacy, for her correction, for her destruction. She appeared in our skin via tattoo artists' needles in fine linework or jailhouse blue-black ink, and in natural formations of rock or wood, or food, or works of art that predated by centuries her existence on this earth.

In a pull-off along the beach near Big Sabine Point, in late September, she appears behind the tinted windows of a black tour bus parked jackknife style with her pony car in tow. Some of us have been waiting here for hours, talking, hugging, sharing our food stores. Others who've made camp overnight in the nearby dunes stream down to stand at attention. At high noon, a hatch opens in the roof of the bus and a ripple of anticipation runs through us as a single hand comes out and grips the rung fixed there and then another, golden, does the same, and the Governor climbs out and strides across the panels of the roof to our cheers, her hands sailing out at her sides like any minute she will take off and fly, and her name is chanted and now her golden arm is raised to the sky and on it are engraved scenes of our history and of triumphs yet to come, and Leona is squeezing me and we're stomping our feet in the shell and gunning the engines of dirt bikes and four-wheelers and beating the horns of cars as she walks on, pumping her fist, and the sun roars overhead.

Acknowledgments

This novel and its author are forever indebted to the following artists:

Leiji Matsumoto

Masamune Shirow

Yoshikazu Yasuhiko

Rumiko Takahashi

Kenichi Sonoda

Yoshihisa Tagami

Ryoichi Ikegami

Haruhiko Mikimoto

Hideaki Anno

Hiromu Arakawa

Shoji Kawamori

Katsuhiro Otomo

Satoshi Kon

In addition to these lifelong sources of inspiration, I would like to thank Emily Burns, whose editorial vision and skills shaped this book more than I can say; Peter Blackstock for reading early, monstrous versions and for putting up with me throughout the process of writing this book; and everyone at Grove Atlantic, whose support has been the greatest gift of my career; Gail Hochman and the team at Brandt & Hochman; my colleagues and students in the Creative Writing program and the Department of English at Old Dominion University; my oldest, dearest friend, Andrew Smith, for years of conversation and the reading of countless drafts; my wife, Alise, the first and best editor and my whole entire heart; and, finally, my daughter, Rosemary, who said I should write a book about cowboys and a girl with a robot arm.